THE GIRLS OF CANBY HALL

PARTY TIME!

EMILY CHASE

SCHOLASTIC INC.
New York Toronto London Auckland Sydney

ISBN 0-590-40657-4

12 11 10 9 8 7 6 5 4 3 2 1   7 8 9/8 0 1 2/9

Printed in the U.S.A.
First Scholastic printing, April 1987

THE GIRLS OF CANBY HALL

PARTY TIME!

THE GIRLS
OF CANBY HALL

21

CHAPTER ONE

"Hurry up, you two!" Andy Cord shouted back up the snow-covered steps of their dorm, Baker House, where her roommates — Jane Barrett and Toby Houston — were making tentative steps down, like goats on the side of a mountain.

A huge January snowstorm was raging around them, sweeping across the campus of Canby Hall school for girls, in Greenleaf, Massachusetts. Andy, who came from Chicago and was always boasting about what rough weather she was used to, was leading the way, trying to seem brave and hearty.

"Slowpokes!" she teased them.

"We're coming as fast as we can," Jane said. "I'm trying to not drop this stupid cake. And Toby's never been in a snowstorm. She's scared."

Andy turned and saw Toby baby-stepping along the snow-drifted path in her cowboy boots. The sight made Andy burst out laughing, and then she couldn't resist teasing.

"Toby Houston! Intrepid rider of the purple sage. Star of the junior rodeo circuit. The Texas Terror — afraid of a few little snowflakes?!"

"Come on, Andy," Jane pleaded. "Give the poor girl a break. I've lived my whole life here in Massachusetts and I've never seen a snowstorm like this. And I don't recall seeing anything like this last week in the Windy City." The three of them had spent the past week of Christmas break in Chicago, helping out in Andy's family's restaurant.

"Well," Andy said, "I guess I have to admit this *is* about the most snow I've ever seen in one place at one time. Maybe the weather's in league with us. Maybe it's trying to snow Alison in so she can't leave."

"Wouldn't that be great!" Toby said, her curly red hair covered with snow. "I still can't really believe she's leaving for good tomorrow."

"*I* still can't really believe we're ever going to make it to the dining hall to say good-bye to her," Jane said, pulling the collar of her cashmere coat up around her neck.

The three roommates of 407 Baker House were very, *very* different fifteen-year-olds. Jane was a rich society girl from Boston; Andy an outgoing urban black girl from Chicago; and Toby a fiercely independent girl from a ranch in Texas. But one thing they were in total agreement on was Alison Cavanaugh. They all thought she was the greatest possible housemother in the world. Maybe in the universe.

Alison had gotten married at Thanksgiving, and now she was leaving Canby Hall to live with her husband, David, and start graduate school in Boston. All the girls of Baker House dorm were sad about losing her. Alison had been more friend than housemother to most of them — always there with a smile or a hug or a shoulder to cry on, and usually with a plate of cookies thrown in for good measure. The only problem was that these were usually the healthy-type cookies Alison believed in — made of oats and groats and carob and wheat germ and things like that. Alison was kind of a belated hippie. She was big on health foods, and played Indian sitar music records and old Beatles albums, and wore only natural fiber clothes. Everyone agreed that Alison was different but great. No one would be able to replace her in their hearts. But someone *was* going to replace her in her job, and in her top-floor apartment, which everyone called The Penthouse. All that the girls knew so far about Alison's replacement was her name. Meredith Pembroke.

"I wonder what this Pembroke turkey's going to be like? I hear Alison's going to introduce her at the farewell party tonight,"

Andy said. They were walking in a kind of huddle now for warmth, their arms around each other's shoulders.

"We don't know for sure that she's a turkey," Jane said. "You're just letting your allegiance to Alison get in the way. Meredith Pembroke could very well be a lovely person. It's a lovely name."

"I wonder what they call her for short?" said Toby, whose own nickname was a shortening of October, the month she was born in. "Merrie?"

"Pemmy?" Jane suggested.

"Brokey?" Andy said, which for some reason cracked them all up.

Nearly everyone else from Baker House was already in the dining hall when Andy, Toby, and Jane finally got there. The girls from the third floor were in the middle of a skit poking fun at Alison's weak points as a housemother. Cindy Fredericks was impersonating Alison in a long reddish wig and big horn-rimmed glasses. She was lying down under a comforter while one of the other girls pretended to knock on the door.

"What is it?" Cindy/Alison shouted, sitting up and looking blearily around.

"I-I-I have a problem," the girl sobbed.

"Are you dying?"

"Dying? Why no."

"Then come back after eleven. The only

problem I could get up this early for would be death."

The whole room went into gales of laughter. Alison, who saw the truth in this satire, laughed and blushed and held her hands over her face. She was sitting on top of one of the dining hall's round wood tables — her seat of honor for the show.

More skits and tributes followed, and the girls gave Alison a great group photo with everyone in Baker posing in punked-up spiky hair and sunglasses. Alison loved it.

When the fourth floor girls took their turn, it was to present Alison with a poem. They had picked Jane to read it because she had a strong voice and didn't trip over words when reading aloud. The other girls got behind her and backed her with a humming chorus, sort of like the music in elevators. Jane began:

"Farewell to you, o Alison.
You were great, but now you're gone.
We'll remember you — no matter where
    you're at.
We'll also recall Doby, your cat.

So don't look back and think of us.
Just get on that Boston bus.
You'll stay in our hearts and be our fave.
Even if you deserted us to marry Dave."

"Alison!" Jane said, looking up from the

poem and over at the housemother with tears streaming down her cheeks. "Are you crying because you're so moved?"

"No," Alison said, starting to laugh. "Because it's such a terrible poem."

Pretty soon, it was time for the cake. Jane got it out of its white cardboard box and set it down in front of Alison so she could cut it. It wasn't really a cake, though. It was actually made out of *papier-mâché* molded around a large rock then painted a truly gruesome greenish-yellowish brown with pink spots. Alison's eyes opened wide in dismay as she looked down at it.

"Alison," Jane said, "we three roommates of 407 have baked this special cake for you. We put in all your favorite foods: blackstrap molasses, brown rice, rose hips, seaweed, and for a festive touch — pink-tinted tofu!"

Alison looked down at this item with great wariness. Andy handed her a knife. "Go ahead. Cut it," she urged.

Alison reluctantly put the knife on the cake and pushed down. To absolutely no effect. She tried harder, sawing away this time, but still nothing happened.

"Uh, how long did you guys leave this in the oven?"

Everyone burst out laughing and Maggie Morrison and Dee Adams, who lived in the room next to Andy, Jane, and Toby, brought out the real thing — a gigantic chocolate cake and cartons of chocolate-chocolate-chip ice cream to go with it. Chocolate was the one food that could get Alison off her health food crusade. She couldn't resist the stuff and all her girls knew it.

"You can use this one as a paperweight for your thesis," Toby told Alison, thudding the fake cake down on the table.

When everyone had finished eating, they started chanting, "Speech, speech, speech."

"I can't give a real speech," Alison said. "I'd break down and cry and make a mess of this wonderful party. All I can say is what you already know. I love Canby Hall. And I'm happy I got to be a part of it. And as much as I'm looking forward to living with David in Boston and going back to school myself, I'm going to miss you and this place like crazy. Oh no. I'm crying, anyway." When someone had passed her a tissue and she had a chance to wipe her eyes and pull herself back together a little, she went on. "This is really a two-part party. Now that the first part — the good-bye-to-me part — is over, I'd like to move on to the happier part — welcoming your new housemother. I hope you all will give her a big round of applause to make her feel right at home here. May I introduce Meredith Pembroke."

From the back of the room, a young woman who looked to be in her late twenties walked briskly to the front where Alison was sitting. She was tall and thin and overdressed for this informal get-together in a navy linen suit with a white blouse and softly bowed scarf-tie at her neck. She was good-looking, but with an extremely severe set to her jaw and steel in her large gray eyes. Her dark hair was pulled back and tied in a knot at the back of her neck. She was pretty much the exact opposite of Alison. Her manner did nothing to inspire warmth in the girls, but to be polite, they clapped until she came up next to Alison and raised her hands to quiet the room.

"Thank you, girls," she said. "As Alison told you, my name is Ms. Pembroke. I'm looking forward to serving as your housemother and getting to know each of you on a one-to-one basis. Tomorrow, I will post a schedule of my hours for appointments. . . ."

Andy turned to Jane and mouthed "appointments?" as Meredith went on. "Now, as my first act as new housemother, I'm afraid I must point out that it's Thursday night — a weeknight — which means ten-thirty curfew. We are already — " she looked at her watch " — seventeen minutes past that. Since this is technically a school function, I won't give anyone a demerit for being here, but I do want you all to begin cleaning up, saying good-night to Alison, and heading back to Baker House. I think fifteen minutes ought to be enough time. For anyone coming in after that, I'm afraid I'll have to give late minutes."

And with that she walked out of the room.

The entire room was silent in the wake of her departure. The girls looked to Alison for help, but she could only shrug and say, "People have different styles. You may have to do a little adapting to adjust to Mer — I mean Ms. Pembroke. She sees this position a little differently than I have. She sees the dormitory as a slightly different kind of place."

"Yeah," Andy shouted, speaking for nearly every girl in the room, "kind of like a maximum security, federal prison kind of place."

At least this got a laugh and broke through the gloom and put them all back into enough of a good mood to say their final farewells to Alison.

On the way back across campus — where the snowstorm had died down to fat wet flakes falling softly in the lights along the pathways — the three roommates of 407 Baker had a talk about the new housemother.

"What's with her, do you think?" Andy said. "I mean, is she for real?"

"Maybe she's just putting on a tough front at first so everyone won't walk all over her," Toby said optimistically.

"Maybe," Jane said, but with little conviction in her voice. "But I think we should probably prepare ourselves for the possibility that a golden era is passing with Alison's leaving, and that Baker House may be entering a new phase. The Alcatraz phase."

CHAPTER TWO

Eeeeeeeee!!!" screamed Jane in pure delight as the toboggan shot down the side of Edgar Hill. As they picked up speed, she clung even tighter to her boyfriend, Cary, who was riding in the front spot. Meanwhile, Jane's own ribs were being crushed and her left eardrum split by Andy, who was sitting behind her, hanging on, screaming for dear life.

Andy herself sat enfolded in the arms of her almost, sort-of, maybe boyfriend Matt. (It was too soon for her to tell if this was going to be true love, or just a flash in the pan.) Behind Matt, taking up the last two spots on the toboggan, were Toby and her friend Randy Crowell.

Nobody around Greenleaf remembered who Edgar had been, but the hill named after him was where you'd find most of the teenage population any day the snow was white and heavy on the ground. This particular sunny Sunday after the big snowstorm, the slope was filled with speeding toboggans and sleds and saucer disks.

The six friends didn't quite get a full ride this time. About two-thirds of the way down, they hit a bump that sent Toby and Randy off the back. Then, near the bottom, the toboggan came to a fishtail stop and everyone but Cary slid off into snowbanks.

"The captain always goes down with his ship," he said, dragging the toboggan behind him as he came back to fetch his crew. He gave Jane a hand as she rubbed the side of the leg she'd landed on.

"I'm trying to figure out what I can wear to classes tomorrow. I mean, what goes particularly well with black and blue?"

"Wow!" Cary said. "What a great song that would make — 'The Black and Blues.' About some guy who fell off his toboggan the same day his girl left him."

Cary saw a lot of life as material for songs. He was the lead singer and guitarist in Ambulance — the best band at Oakley Prep, the boys' school down the road from Canby Hall.

If they ran a contest for Least Likely Couple at either school, Jane and Cary would win hands down. She was tall and blond and dressed in the preppie uniforms — shirts with alligators and turtlenecks with little ducks. He was short and had scraggly hair that came to a tail in the back. He wore an earring in one ear and usually walked around with Walkman headphones on both of them. He wore sunglasses around the clock.

Both Jane and Cary came from rich, old Boston families, but whereas he had rebelled against his background, she was enraptured with hers. Jane really loved being a Barrett, loved having one of the oldest, most important names in Boston.

Until she'd met Cary, she had gone for years and years with a guy who thought very much like she did — Cornelius Worthington III. Neal. Why she wasn't going with him anymore and why she *was* going with Cary Slade was still something of a mystery to her. Maybe it was true that opposites attract. All she knew was that when Cary walked into a room — even though it probably meant they would be fighting about something within five minutes — she always felt this kind of quick thuddy thing happen to her heart.

With Neal she had talked about sailing and parties and which schools they'd go to and how servants should be dealt with. They had nearly always seen eye-to-eye. But with Neal, she had never once felt anything thuddy happen to her heart. She realized that what she and Neal had really been all along was friends.

And the amazingly good and unexpected thing that had happened was that she had managed to keep him as a friend even after they'd broken up and she'd started going with Cary. She thought Neal was a truly exceptional guy. She wished she could find a girlfriend for him who would appreciate just how special he was.

Jane and Cary went back to find Andy and Matt, who were brushing the snow off themselves about a hundred feet up the hill. The four of them shielded their eyes against the blinding sun bouncing off the snow and looked up to see Toby and Randy, half running, half shoe-skiing as they held onto each other, coming down the hill.

Randy was older than the rest of them. He was twenty and out of school. He worked on his family's horse ranch, and his friendship with Toby was based a lot on their mutual interest in horses and riding. At first, Toby's interest had also been based on finding Randy terrific-looking and fun and incredibly easy to be with. All the things she would want in a boyfriend. But the differences in their ages was too much, at least for now, at least for him. He treated her like a kid sister. At first this had bothered Toby, but lately she'd been enjoying him more and more as a friend. Today he had passed them in his old pickup truck as they were dragging the toboggan down the road out to the hill. He'd offered a ride and, on the way, they had persuaded him to come along.

* * *

When all six of the toboggan-wreck survivors were together again, Matt and Andy — with dead-giveaway grins on their faces — pulled well-packed snowballs from behind their backs and started a snowball fight that lasted half an hour and left all of them in a state of total collapse.

"How are we ever going to make it back to school?" Andy moaned, lying on her side in the snow as if she were just going to drop off for a little nap right there and then.

"I'll give everyone a lift. We can put your toboggan in the bed of my pickup, Cary," Randy offered.

He was also saving a surprise for everyone — a big thermos of hot apple cider from the trees on the Crowell farm. He passed around Styrofoam cups, and as he drove them home, everyone sat in the back of the truck and drank cider and huddled together in a gathering of down jackets and friendship and corny old singalong songs like "Winter Wonderland."

When they got to the gates of the Canby Hall campus, the girls hopped out and waved good-bye to the guys and began making their slow, tired, happy way back to Baker House.

"I've got something special I want to talk with you about," Jane said when they were midway through the maple grove.

"You and Cary are getting married next weekend in a punk ceremony and you want us to dye our hair purple and be your brides-maids," Andy said. When Jane gave her a fish-eye look, she said, "Well, it was just a guess."

"You're on the right track, though," Jane admitted. "I do want you two to help me celebrate something very special in my life."

"Shoot," Toby said.

"Well, in a couple of weeks it will be time for the Barretts' Landing party."

"The *what*?" Andy said.

"Three hundred years ago, the first Barretts arrived here on the shores of Massachusetts, and so to commemorate the event, my parents are having a big party at our house in Boston."

"Why do I have the distinct feeling this is not going to be a rec room kind of thing where your folks throw on a few records and set out the chips and everybody cuts loose?" Andy said.

An exasperated look crossed Jane's face, but she plunged in again.

"No, it's not going to be *quite* that kind of party. It'll be a slightly more formal affair. Mother and Father will have a small orchestra and serve champagne and hors d'oeuvres. The *crème de la crème* of Boston society will be there. You know what I mean — people whose families have known each other for genera-tions. People whose forefathers came over on the same ships."

"I'll bet they weren't the same ships *my*

forefathers came over on," Andy said sarcastically.

"Oh Andy, come on," Jane said. "There'll be other black people there. One of my mother's best friends is the curator of African art at the museum. She'll be there with her husband. And one of the investment analysts at my father's bank always comes. This is the modern age. Society isn't stodgy anymore. You'll feel perfectly comfortable, I'm sure."

"Will there be many ranch hands there?" Toby asked in a very small voice.

"Will you two just relax! You act like you've never been anywhere. It isn't like I'm asking you to go to a foreign country with bizarre customs. Just a simple weekend at my home with my family and a little party Saturday night. You act like you don't know which fork to use for the escargot, or how to waltz. *Really.*" As she sighed and went on ahead, the other two looked at each other in total bewilderment.

"Waltz?" Andy muttered under her breath.

"Escar — what?" Toby said.

Jane looked at them in despair.

"Are you two just trying to be impossible?" she shouted, then ran on ahead of them, out of the woods.

Toby and Andy stopped and looked at each other. They didn't want to disappoint Jane. Having lived together since September, they had learned that being roommates meant a lot of going out of their ways for one another. Sometimes this meant big things — helping Andy at her family's restaurant, stopping Toby from running away in a burst of home-sickness. But it also meant lots of little things — taking care of each other in day-to-day ways, making sure that 407 Baker was always a warm, safe haven from the sometimes cold, lonely, and stormy life at boarding school.

And so, even if Andy and Toby couldn't get excited about some long-gone relatives of Jane's hopping off a boat here three hundred years ago, even if they didn't know a waltz from a fox trot, or an escargot from a bowl of oatmeal — they knew they had to go to the party for Jane's sake.

"Let's go find her," Toby said.

Andy nodded and they ran off together. They found her up in 407, facedown on her bed. She wasn't making a sound, but they could tell from her shaking shoulders that she was crying.

"Hey Jane," Toby said.

"Don't cry," Andy said, and they both sat down on her bed, edging her over.

"We were just fooling around," Andy said. "Of course we want to come to the party."

"And don't worry about us embarrassing you," Toby added. "I'm going to the library tomorrow and getting out one of those books of etiquette. I'm going to learn up on high society manners."

Jane rolled over and wiped the tears from her eyes as she smiled up at them.

"Yeah," Andy reassured her. "You'll be proud of us." She tried to fill her voice with conviction, but it was all fake. At the moment, she couldn't imagine how she and Toby were going to make it through this party.

Later that night, Andy was still worried about the party and the weekend in Boston. She needed to talk with someone who would understand her fears. Someone who knew the special problems that faced a black girl at a mostly white school like Canby Hall. She needed to talk with Faith Thompson.

Faith had lived in 407, with Dana Morrison and Shelley Hyde, for the three years before Andy came to Canby Hall, so Andy felt a kind of link with her — as though she'd come before and paved the way a little.

She had met Faith over the Thanksgiving weekend when Faith had come in from college for Alison's wedding. The two of them had gotten off to a rough start with each other, but were good friends by the time Faith had left. Andy looked up to her. And if anyone would know how to handle this fancy party situation, it would be Faith. She was one of the most sophisticated young women Andy knew. Ultracool. It was hard to imagine a social situation she couldn't handle.

Andy didn't want Jane to know she was

worried and calling Faith, so she came up with a ruse to slip downstairs to the pay phones.

"Argh!" she said, stretching her arms above her as she sat at her desk. The three of them were studying for the next day's classes. "Sometimes I think geometry was invented just to torture me."

"Oh, but think of how valuable it's going to be to you in the long run," Jane said sarcastically. "All the rest of your life, you're going to be able to measure an isosceles triangle."

"It'll do wonders for your social life, too," Toby teased. "When guys come up and ask if you can dance, you'll be able to say, 'Sure — but better yet, watch me figure the area of this parallelogram.' "

Andy laughed imagining this scene, then, putting her lie into action, said, "Hey. Is anybody else hungry? I was thinking about making a little trip down to the machines."

"You could get me a root beer," Jane said, then went back to highlighting in her English book. No one highlighted more than Jane. When she was done with a book, more words were highlighted than un-highlighted. She even used different color highlighters to indicate degree of importance.

"If there are any ice-cream sandwiches, I'll take one," Toby said, lifting her pen from the history essay she was writing on "Accomplishments of the Egyptians."

When Andy got Faith on the phone, she was glad she'd brought all her change. Actually, she was afraid she'd use it all up before she even got her friend on the line. Faith lived in a boarding house near the campus of the university at Rochester and someone else answered the phone, then seemed to take about an hour to go and get her.

"Faith!" Andy said excitedly when she finally heard Faith's voice on the other end.

"Hey girl!" Faith said, recognizing Andy's instantly. "What a surprise!"

"I've got a problem," Andy said, "and you're the only one I can really talk to about it." She went on to explain about the party and her fears of seeming odd and out of place at it.

Faith listened with a lot of attention, then said, "But you say there're supposed to be other blacks there."

"Yeah, but give me a break — a museum curator and some megabanker. Maybe Eddie Murphy's going to turn up as a surprise guest. Just regular folks. And aside from them, you can bet that party's going to be a sea of white faces. And worse, they're all going to be society types. They're all going to have manners I haven't even heard of. I'm going to be completely lost. Of course, Toby'll be worse off on that score than I will, even. Her idea of manners is not putting your boots up on the table until everyone's done eating."

Faith's laughter traveled across the miles. "You two should probably get hold of one of those etiquette guides."

"Toby's checking that out at the library."

"Good. And as for you in particular, Andrea Cord — remember what they used to say in the sixties. Black is beautiful! It's still true."

Andy smiled at how sincerely Faith was trying to boost her confidence.

"And another thing," Faith said, on a roll now, "If I could go to Iowa with Shelley — to Pine Bluff, where a black person is practically rare enough to attract small crowds on street corners — you can go to one little bitty Boston blueblood party."

"Thanks, Faith. I needed that," Andy kidded over her gratitude.

"It was nothing. What are friends for, anyway? Just be sure to call me when you get back. I've got a feeling some great stories are going to come out of this Boston weekend."

Andy was full of good feeling when she hung up the phone. She turned and started to head for the machines in the Ping-Pong room, to get Toby and Jane their treats, when she was stopped in her tracks by a crisp voice.

"Just a minute, please."

It was Meredith Pembroke, dressed in yet another business suit, holding a small pad of pink paper. She was filling out the top sheet.

"Name, please?" she said coolly.

"Andy . . . uh, Andrea Cord. But what is this?"

"I'm sure you're aware that calls are not permitted after eleven o'clock lights-out."

"But eleven is when the rates go down," Andy said. "Everyone makes their long distance calls then."

"Then everyone will get demerit slips, I'm afraid," Meredith Pembroke said, continuing to write.

"Demerit slips?!" Andy started laughing. "Oh, Mer . . . Ms. Pembroke. Those are kind of a thing of the past around here. Alison never gave them out."

"Is that right?" Meredith Pembroke said in an eerily calm tone. "Well, Alison isn't housemother here anymore. *I* am. And I go by the book. And I give demerits to those who don't." She pulled the pink slip off the top of the pad and dangled it by a corner in front of Andy's nose until she took it and stomped off furiously.

When she was a few feet down the hall, she heard Ms. Pembroke say, in a voice filled with fake sweetness, "Good-night, Andrea."

CHAPTER THREE

The most flattering way anyone could describe the decor of Room 407 Baker would be "eclectic." Andy, Toby, and Jane had dramatically different personalities, and these were displayed, side-by-side, in the small space of one dorm room. It looked a little like one of those Hollywood backlots where Roman ruins have been pushed up against Western Main Streets, right beside a spaceship.

Jane's section of the room looked like something out of a Victorian novel. Her cross-stitch quilt matched the pastel Persian rug next to her bed. On her nightstand stood an old-fashioned milk-glass lamp. Amid and around and on top of all this were the piles of clothes and makeup and books and coffee mugs and empty soda cans that seemed to grow on Jane's part of the room like moss on a tree.

Andy's bed, against another wall, was neatly covered with a spread that had a bold geometric pattern. On top of that were her "friends" — a collection of stuffed animals so tattered they had to have come from her baby days. On the wall above the bed were two ballet posters: one of a couple in a classical *pas de deux,* the other a close-up of a pair of dancer's tired-out feet in worn toe shoes, bulky legwarmers sliding down around the ankles. "The fantasy and the reality" was how Andy described the posters.

Being a first-rate ballet dancer was Andy's single overriding ambition. She was determined to make it against all the odds. She filled most of her nonschool time with ballet and modern dance classes, and with hours and hours of floor exercises. Even her dreams at night were filled with fantasies of herself fluttering across some unnamed stage in the lead role in *Giselle.*

While Andy was dreaming of dancing in front of the footlights, Toby would be across the room, sleeping deeply as she rode her old horse, Max, across the Texas of her dreams. She, too, knew what she wanted to be when she grew up — a rancher like her father. She read any book she could find about brave pioneer women, and was always happy when *The Big Valley* went into reruns so she could watch Barbara Stanwyck run that ranch of hers with an iron hand.

Her part of the room really looked like a bunkhouse. Her bed had the plain standard issue Canby Hall sheets (which Andy joked weren't white, but that new ultrafashionable color, Shadow Gray) and an old green army blanket. On her desk was a two-sided picture frame. In one side was a picture of her father, in the other a photo of her horse, Max. Toby's mother had died several years before. When Jane had asked why she didn't have her mother's picture out, Toby had said it would be too painful.

The only other item of decor, if you could call it that, in Toby's part of the room was the mysterious tea bag she had taped to the ceiling above her bed the night she'd arrived. She had never explained this to anyone and ignored anyone who asked about it. By now, Toby's tea bag had become one of the minor mysteries of Baker House.

Monday after classes, all three girls were in the room. Andy was on the floor, doing some stretching exercises. Toby was studying her biology textbook. She was making out three-by-five cards on the major human bones.

"You could highlight those cards," Jane suggested. "Blue for major bones, yellow for minor ones. You know."

"Yeah," Toby said, ducking. "Great idea. I'll think about it."

Jane was getting ready to go out with Cary for pizza. She was planning to spring an invi-

tation on him to the Barretts' Landing party.
She knew he was in his mellowest possible
mood when he was full of pizza.

"I have to be devious," she told Toby and
Andy as she pulled on a heavy cable-knit ski
sweater. It was powder blue and contrasted
just right with her designer jeans. "He's really
not going to want to go to this. He hates Boston society, thinks of himself as an escapee
from it. And here I am, asking him to take a
dive right into it again."

"So, do you think he'll do it?" Toby asked,
watching Jane pull on a burgundy down vest
over her sweater, then lift her long blond hair
out over the stand-up collar. The other two
envied Jane her clothes. She had about as
many as both of them combined. She was gen-
erous about lending, but it didn't do them
much good, as she was taller than Andy and
a size bigger than Toby.

"I hope so," Jane said. "I'm counting on
convincing him that this party is an important
event. You know, the Barretts are really part
of the heritage of this country. It was a Barrett — David French Barrett — who gave Paul
Revere a fresh horse along the way of his
famous Midnight Ride."

"Isn't that your dad's name?" Toby asked.

"Yes. All the firstborn Barrett sons are
named David French Barrett. There were Barretts all over the place in American history.
There was a Barrett — James Owen Barrett

— among the men dumping English tea at the Boston Tea Party."

Andy got an impish look in her eyes and said, "I heard it was another Barrett — Gus Barrett — who was at the writing of the Declaration of Independence. After the other guys signed, he took it out to be photocopied." She burst out laughing at her joke, and got a giggle out of Toby, but Jane just looked at her in stony silence.

Then Jane said, "I don't see why you want to make fun of my ancestors, Andy. Being a Barrett is probably the most important thing in life to me."

Andy muttered, "Sorry," and looked down at the floor. She hadn't meant to insult Jane, only to tease her a little. But apparently this wasn't a subject open to teasing.

"It's okay," Jane told her. "I think you just didn't understand. Now wish me luck with Cary," she said, as she pulled on a pink cashmere beret and mittens, and disappeared out the door.

"Go get him," Toby called after her, then looked across the room at her roommate.

"Well," Andy said, getting off her bed and stretching, "I guess those of us who can't afford to eat out have no choice but to descend into the depths of Hell's Kitchen."

"What's on the menu tonight?" Toby asked.

"The printout on the bulletin board said 'Fisherman's Catch.'"

"Oh no," Toby moaned, and rolled back and forth on the floor. "That probably means old boiled tire."

Making jokes about the food in the Canby Hall dining hall — Hell's Kitchen to the girls — was their best defense against it.

"Well, let's see if Maggie and Dee want to go with us," Andy said. "I hear there's safety in numbers. If Fisherman's Catch turns out to be a live octopus, four of us ought to be able to wrestle it to the ground."

Maggie Morrison, Dana's younger sister, and Dee Adams, a blond California girl, shared the room next to Andy's.

In the dining hall, seated around one of the smaller wooden tables, Toby, Andy, Dee, and Maggie all stared down bleakly at their plates.

"Come on, you guys," Maggie said. She was always an optimist. "It's probably fish. Of some kind."

"It's definitely something from the sea," Dee — who was always sarcastic — added. "I can tell from the smell."

"At least it's covered with a lot of this greenish sauce," Andy said. "So you can't really get too specific about what it is exactly. Somehow I think that's for the best."

Toby didn't say anything. She was already

halfway through hers. The others looked at her in amazement.

"Tobe," Dee said. "You are truly astonishing. A real goat. I've been eating with you since September and I haven't seen anything from those steam tables that's stopped you in your tracks yet."

"Actually," Toby protested, "this stuff's not all that bad."

The others groaned, but lifted their forks and started in.

"At least we'll probably get decent food at the Barrett house," Andy grumbled.

"You going to visit Jane's family?" Dee asked.

Andy explained about the party, and then about her and Toby's fears about it.

"Boy, I'd love to go and stick my tongue out at all those hoity-toity snobs," Dee said. She was much more into the modern than the traditional.

"Well, so would we, but —" Andy started to say, but was interrupted by Maggie.

"Hey. What's purple with green spots and sort of shakes?"

"I give," Toby said.

"The dessert," Maggie replied, poking at the jiggly square.

"As I was *saying*" — Andy tried to get the conversation back on track — "Toby and I would dearly love to go to this party and be outrageous, but we can't embarrass Jane."

"Maybe she'd like to stick *her* tongue out at all that high society stuff, too," Dee said.

"Oh no," Toby replied, "that's the worst part. She wouldn't. She really thinks it's all so neat. She thinks *everything* about the Barretts is fascinating, and that being a part of the upper crust is extremely cool."

"You could tell her you don't agree," Maggie suggested.

"Yeah," Dee added. "Why not? Just tell her this whole thing is not your style and you don't really want to go."

"We can't," Toby said dismally. "It'd be like me inviting you all to come home with me, and you all just casually telling me no thanks, Texas was for the birds. You just wouldn't do that. You'd know it was too important to me. Well, this is the same thing. No, I think we've just got to give it the old Canby Hall try. I got this etiquette book out of the library today. I'm going to study up and by the time we get to the Barretts' house, Andy and I are going to know exactly how to mind our p's and q's."

"Give us an example," Dee urged. "From the book. See if we're a mannerly bunch."

"Well, it says that at formal dinners, one should use the outside fork first and work inward toward the plate for each successive course."

"Oh, just like here!" Maggie exclaimed, picking a French fry off her plate. "I've always felt one should use the outside fingers to pick up the fry. Unless they are of the ultra-greasy variety served on these premises. Then I feel one must really resort to using *all* the fingers."

Everyone laughed, but Andy thought to herself that she and Toby probably weren't going to be having the last laugh when they were sitting at the Barrett dining table.

CHAPTER FOUR

"Another glass, please, of your vintage root beer," Cary was saying to the waitress as he lifted his empty glass.

Jane had been having such a good time with him at Pizza Pete's that she was shying away from mentioning the Barretts' Landing party. Cary was sure to hate the idea. He would absolutely refuse to go and then she'd have to spend a couple of hours trying to talk him into it. This was what she'd had to do to get him to come to Alison's wedding. And maybe this time she wouldn't be able to talk him into it. Maybe they'd just get into a huge, irresolvable fight.

When they were out of the restaurant, Cary suggested they go back to his dorm. Oakley Prep held a Monday night open house once a month. The boys could have friends and girlfriends up in their rooms — as long as they left the doors open. It was a way for Oakley guys to entertain in their own space, and to introduce their friends to their roommates. Cary shared a room with a guy named Stu Price, who was tall and gangly and spoke mainly in monosyllables, when he spoke at all.

"He does all his real talking with computers," Cary told Jane once. And Stu did seem to spend most of his time in the computer science lab. Which was fine with Jane. When he *was* around, he usually sat off to the side, not studying, but not saying anything to her, either. Mostly he just sat there looking like he *might* say something, which unnerved Jane considerably.

"Stu's okay," Cary always assured her, but she had her doubts.

"Maybe on *his* planet he's okay. But here on Earth, he's a little weird."

"He's real shy," Cary said. "Just being around us, even without talking, is about as social as he gets."

This piece of information helped Jane to understand Stu's silences, but it didn't make him any easier to be around. And she was relieved when, on the way down the hall toward Cary's room that night, he mentioned, "Stu's at the lab. So you two won't be able to chat up a storm like you usually do. I always feel so left out."

"Ha, ha," she said as they turned into his room.

Now that Jane had gotten beyond worrying about the million other differences between her and Cary, the one great remaining obstacle to them living happily ever after was that he was a neatness freak and she was a total slob.

She had lived her whole life before Canby Hall being waited on and picked up after by servants. And so she simply had no concept of keeping things in order around herself. Toby and Andy put up with her and, when things got completely out of control, they sort of shoveled her things into a heap by her bed so she'd have to do something about it or not be able to sleep that night.

But Cary! He was the model of neatness. He folded his T-shirts and underwear into squares, then stacked them by color in his drawers. He lined up his paper clips on the edge of his desk. The books on his shelf were in alphabetical order.

"Oh, I see you don't use the Dewey decimal system," Jane had teased him the first time she was there, but what she had really been thinking was, We are so different.

And so she had never even mentioned her true slob nature to him. But every time she came into his room, her heart sank.

"Notice anything?" he asked that night.

She looked around, but couldn't see what he was referring to.

"I give."

"I figured out how to make hospital corners on my bed. See? Now you really can bounce a dime off — like in the Marines." He demonstrated.

"It's really kind of funny," she pointed out to him. "Here you are, this big-time rebel against the establishment, but secretly you're neater than my mother."

"Well," he said, "I was neat *before* I was a rebel. My neatness goes way back with me. I used to win all those coloring contests. You know, where they wanted you to stay inside the lines. I think a lot of the ways we are now, we already were even when we were really little. A lot of the things that were important to us then stay important all our lives."

Seeing her opening, Jane thought this was probably the best opportunity she was likely to have that night to bring up The Difficult Question. And so she dove in.

"Oh, you're so right. Like with me, it's my family. Ever since I was really little, I've known I'm a Barrett, linked through the past to all these Barretts before me. I can't imagine ever growing away from my family, or not caring about them. Or not getting really excited about the Barretts' Landing party."

"You want to listen to the new Del Fuegos record I got?" he asked, showing her the album jacket, gliding over what she'd just said.

"Were you listening to me?" she asked, upset. "Did you hear what I said?"

"Sure. You said you're all excited about the Barrett sanding party. What's that — a beach kind of thing? You and your folks and Charlotte go down to Florida?"

"Landing!" Jane found herself shouting. "Barretts' *Landing* party! It's to celebrate the arrival of the very first Barretts here in Massachusetts three hundred years ago." She was really angry now, and getting even angrier as she anticipated the attack he was about to make on her family and their way of life.

But that's not what happened. Instead, he got an excited gleam in his eye and said, "Is this going to be a big party?"

She nodded.

"All those high-society types your parents hang out with?"

She nodded again.

"And those Ivy League pals of your sister?"

"Yes," Jane said, now suspecting some kind of sneak attack. But what he said was, "Great! Can I come? Please?!"

"What?"

"Can I come? Will you bring me along?"

"B-b-but why?" she stammered, not believing her ears.

"Well, in my anthropology class, Mr. Burton wants us to do a study of a cultural rite. He says you don't have to go to some remote island to find tribal rituals, that our society is full of them. What could be a more interesting ritual to put under the old microscope than your family's party?"

Jane was so furious she couldn't speak, she could only glare at Cary.

"Oh no," he said, sincerely. "I didn't insult you, did I?"

"Oh no," she said sarcastically. "Of course not. You as much as say my relatives are a bunch of squiggly worms and I'm supposed to be thrilled that you're going to drop by and dissect them."

"Come on, Jane," he pleaded. "You have to see how interesting this ancestor worship thing is. I could do a really great paper on it."

"Ancestor worship?! I can't believe you're saying this. How insensitive can you be?" she said. When she had come into the room, she had slid her mittens and hat and down vest off onto one of the desk chairs. Now she started to put them all back on again. But Cary grabbed her arm before she finished.

"Wait just one minute!" he insisted. "Are you forgetting how we met? The dance where Ambulance was playing? If my memory's right, you came to that for precisely the same reason — to write an essay on 'an unusual experience.' And I had to stand up on that stage, playing the music I believe in, watching you take those furious little notes of yours — and then highlighting them! Like the band was some sort of curiosity, some carnival sideshow act. I just don't think, after that, you dare have any objections to me coming to have a look at the Barretts at play."

He let go of her arm and they stood there in the middle of the room in a silent stand-off. He had her dead-to-rights and she knew it. She just couldn't bring herself to give in on the point.

Into the middle of this tense little scene Stu sauntered in, carrying a file box of floppy disks and trailing a sheaf of printouts over his arm. When he had carefully set all this down on his desk — he and Cary had been matched up as roommates because each had listed "neatness" as their first priority — he sat down and assumed his usual cheerful but silent stare.

At this particular moment, this was the last straw for Jane. She looked at them both with exasperation and exploded, "Boys! Argh!"

And with that, she stomped out of the room.

Meanwhile, back in 407 Baker, Toby was contemplating herself in the mirror on the back of the door while Andy, Maggie, and Dee sat on the floor playing a game of Clue.

"Do you think I'd look hipper if I got my hair cut real short with the top standing straight up, like Marni Chester's?"

"Marni Chester is a turkey," Dee said. "I think she has someone make sure she's got matching socks on in the morning. I've always thought she got that cut to simplify combing for herself. So I'd say if you can manage to comb all the hair you've got now, you ought to keep it that way."

"I think Marni Chester's hair is cute," Maggie said, then added, "I think Colonel Mustard did it with the revolver in the billiard room."

"Well," Dee said, showing Maggie the Colonel Mustard card cupped in her hands so Andy wouldn't see it, too, "if you do get that cut, be sure to do it before Jane's party. I want you to make just the right impression on her family." Dee thought the Barretts' Landing party was completely stupid, and that Jane had gone completely round the bend on the subject of her family.

"Shhh," Toby said, hearing familiar footsteps coming down the hall. She poked her head out the door and, sure enough, it was Jane. She could tell from the look on her roommate's face that something was wrong.

"Cary said no," she guessed, putting a hand on Jane's shoulder as she passed into the room.

"Worse," Jane said cryptically.

"He *will* go, but only if he can come dressed as Benedict Arnold," Maggie said. She knew she was treading on thin ice, but thought maybe she could kid Jane into a better mood.

It didn't work. Jane ignored the remark and just stood there peeling her clothes off, letting them drop to the floor around her, not bothering to put them away. Then she burrowed around in the small mountain of things on her bed and found her long nightshirt and slipped it over her head. The others, figuring this meant she wanted to be left alone, went back to their Clue game.

"I think it was done by Miss Scarlet with the lead pipe in the conservatory," Andy said.

"How can you care about Clue at a time like this?!" Jane burst out. "I and my whole family and all my ancestors have just been insulted by my boyfriend, and all you three care about is Miss Scarlet and Colonel Mustard. Well, thank you very much. I guess I'll take my problems down to the broom closet and work them out by myself."

Before they could jump in with protests, she was gone. They listened to her footsteps recede down the hall. The broom closet was about the only place on the floor where a girl could get guaranteed privacy. There was only room enough in it, among the mops and buckets and vacuum cleaners, for one person. That person was usually some fourth-floor girl with a worry, or a case of homesickness, or heartbreak. Tonight the girl in the broom closet was going to be Jane.

Dee broke the silence by asking Andy and Toby, "Can't you guys get her down off her high horse? I don't know if I can stand to listen to much more of this."

They shook their heads. Andy spoke for both of them.

"If we ever could have, we've missed our chance by now. Jane's got way too much momentum going on this party. I think we just have to grin and bear it until those Barretts land."

CHAPTER FIVE

Dear Faith,
Why is it time seems to travel at least twice its regular speed at Canby Hall? I can hardly believe it's been two weeks since I called you.

I thought you might be interested in an update on the "Embarrassed Landing" party (what Toby and I have started to call it). Jane has pretty much gone off the deep end on the whole thing. Once in a while she actually speaks a normal sentence on some other subject, but mostly she just sounds like a prerecorded historical message service. For instance, you may not be aware that, in addition to having been biggies in the world of government, the Barretts were also heavily involved in the world of sports.

Amanda Barrett won one of the first big titles in women's amateur tennis in 18-something or other. Seems wherever you look, those Barretts just keep popping up, doing the most surprising and wonderful things. The funny thing is, before this stupid party and all the hoopla around it, I didn't have one bad thought about the Barretts. But by now I have been driven to the point of wishing some skeleton would tumble out of their closet. Surely there must've been a rotten apple in that barrel. Maybe Lizzie Barrett, who bumped off her whole family of Barretts.

What Toby and I are mostly hoping now is that this is only temporary insanity on Jane's part, that after the party she'll go back to being her regular Jane-like self. We're biting our tongues and hoping we can hold out that long. And that we can make it through the party without doing something hopelessly wrong. We're reading the etiquette book every night and now know stuff like how to introduce a younger person to an older person and how to curtsy before royalty. (Don't laugh, there might be some there.)

The one part Toby and I are both looking forward to is seeing Boston. Neither of us has ever been there. Jane's going to be busy helping her mother with the party, but Cary is supposed to show us the sights.

I'll call as soon as I get back and give you all the details. Meanwhile, keep your fingers crossed that we don't fall into the punch bowl.

Love,
Andy

P.S. Meredith Pembroke is reaching new heights (or is it depths?) of awfulness. The other day she gave Heide Fraser a demerit slip for eating a Twinkie in the stairwell. She'd just gotten it out of the basement machines and was on her way up to the third floor. Apparently there's some ancient rule that no one's ever heard of, but it's still on the books from about 1899. It says no food is to be consumed in the halls and stairwells of the dormitories. Meredith specializes in finding these obscure rules and then waiting like a cop in a speed trap to spring a demerit on you.

It's very weird having someone like this for housemother — especially after someone as great as Alison. We all try to tiptoe around her. No one talks to her. I wonder if she ever gets lonely up there in The Penthouse, just her and her rule book. Do you think she has any friends?

CHAPTER SIX

"What kind of car does Cary drive?" Toby asked Andy. She was sitting on the window seat in 407, looking out through a patch she'd rubbed clear on the frost-covered pane.

"A red Toyota," Andy said.

"This is probably him, then," she said, then unlatched the window and opened it to a burst of frigid air. She waited until he emerged from the car and then shouted, "We'll be right down."

He looked up and smiled and made an "okay" sign with a circle of his thumb and index finger.

Jane had taken the train to Boston the day before, to give her mother a hand with last-minute preparations for Saturday's party. Cary had offered to give Toby and Andy a ride to Boston on Friday afternoon, and here he was, right on time at three-thirty.

The two roommates gathered up their luggage and raced down the stairs and out to Cary's car. He hopped out and put their things in the hatchback. Then Toby climbed into the backseat and Andy into the front next to Cary, and they were off. The car was warm and noisy with both the heater and the stereo going full blast. Cary turned down the volume on Tom Petty and the Heartbreakers.

"Funny how a radio that sounds just perfect when you're alone suddenly seems way too loud as soon as someone else gets into the car," he said. "So. You two getting all excited about being tourists in Boston?"

"Oh yeah!" Andy said.

"Jane told us you're going to show us all the sights," Toby said, leaning forward, putting her head through the space between the front seats.

"That's right. *All* the sights," Cary said. "First we'll see the Statue of Liberty. Then we'll go up to the top of the Sears Tower. Then we can take a burrow trip down into the Grand Canyon. And I know you'll both want to see Mt. Rushmore."

"Do you think we'll still have time left over to see the Taj Mahal?" Andy asked, hooking onto his game.

"Absolutely," Cary said. "We'll save that until nighttime. It's prettiest by moonlight, anyway. We can all hide out there through the party. They'll never think of looking for us in the Taj Mahal."

"Jane told us you're going to write the party up for your anthropology class," Toby said. "I guess you know she's not too happy about that. She says you're treating her family like rats in a lab maze."

"But she can't be angry with me because she knows it's exactly what she did to me that first night she came to see Ambulance play. Turnabout is fair play," he said, an impish grin crossing his face.

"Have you met her family?" Andy asked him.

"No," he said. "But I've got a pretty good idea of what to expect. Boston bluebloods tend to have a lot in common."

"Like?"

"Well, they're usually rich and usually in banking or real estate. And they all went to the same schools and go to the same Caribbean islands for vacations. And the men wear their fathers' tweed jackets and the women still use their mother's recipes. It's a place where life stays pretty much the same. Which is what they like best about it."

"Sounds a little dull," Andy mused.

"Oh, I thought it was worse than dull. Much worse. I thought it was suffocating," he said. "Which is why I think the way I do and look like I look now. I figure it ought to give Mr. and Mrs. Barrett at least a little pause

when they see their daughter's new boyfriend."

"Wow, I hadn't thought of that!" Andy
said. "Here Toby and I were only thinking
about *us* embarrassing Jane, coming into her
society world like bulls into a china shop.
We hadn't even thought of her problem bringing someone as weird as *you* home to Mom
and Dad."

"Gee, thanks," he said sarcastically.

"Well, you know what I mean," Andy said.

Cary had to laugh.

"Yeah, I guess I do," he said. "But I figure
we are three terrific persons of the teenage
persuasion, and if the Barretts don't appreciate our winning ways, it's *their* problem."

"Well said," Andy agreed.

"All *right*," Toby chimed in from the back.

"Oooo, the new Lionel Richie song," Andy
said, rolling the volume knob up, drowning
them all in great music as they curved along
the entrance ramp to the interstate to Boston.

"Oh, it's so cute!" Andy exclaimed when
they'd arrived in Boston and were on their way
to Jane's house in Louisburg Square.

"Hey!" Cary said. "I'm not sure how I feel
about you calling my hometown 'cute.'"

"Oh, I meant it as a compliment," Andy
said. "Really."

"Are we at this Louisburg Square yet?"
Toby said, yawning and stretching her way

out of the nap she'd fallen into somewhere
along the way. "And just what *is* Louisburg
Square, anyway?"

"It's really pretty. And one of the best ad-
dresses in Boston. Very historical," he said.
"I'm surprised Jane hasn't told you all about
it."

"If there's history involved, so am I," Andy
said. "I didn't think there was anything about
the Barrett family history — back to those
Cro-Magnon Barretts — that she'd missed
telling us about."

"Here we are," Cary said, rounding a corner
into a cobblestoned street that wrapped
around a little park, asleep for the winter
with a blanket of snow over its grass, the
branches of its elm trees bare. Surrounding
the park was a black iron fence.

"Can you get in there?" Toby asked.

"If you live here you have a key," he said,
waving a hand to indicate the nearly identical
red brick row houses with stone steps and
rounded bays of shuttered windows. "Some
famous people have lived here. Louisa May
Alcott lived in that one there — Number Ten.
And William Dean Howells, who wrote *The
Rise of Silas Lapham*, lived there in Number
Four."

"What a neat thing for Jane," Toby said.
"She wants to be a writer, too. It must make
her feel like she's got history going for her —

that maybe she'll be the next important writer
to come from Louisburg Square."

"How do you know so much about this
place, Cary?" Andy wondered. "Are you a history nut like Jane?"

He laughed.

"No, but when you grow up in Boston, you
kind of have history served to you for breakfast, lunch, and dinner. They put us on those
yellow buses and dragged us off on field trips
to all the local historical sites. I think I came
here on three separate field trips. So I ought
to have a fact or two about Louisburg Square
still kicking around in my head." He paused
to look at the house numbers, then pulled the
car up to the curb. "Well, if I'm not mistaken,
I do believe we have *arrived*."

"This is Jane's house?" Andy pointed to the
one they were sitting in front of.

Cary nodded.

"I'm a little nervous about going in," Toby
admitted.

"Just act like you know what you're doing,"
Cary advised. "That goes for the whole weekend. If you can't do anything else, you can always bluff."

"You're all right, Cary Slade," Andy said,
giving him an affectionate punch in the arm.
"You coming in with us?"

"Not now. Got to see my own parental units
first. I told them I'd be home in time for din-

ner. I'll stop by later tonight. Tell Jane, will
you?"

And so Andy and Toby found themselves all
alone — very alone — on the windswept steps
in front of the imposing front door of Jane's
house. They put down their bags and looked
at each other and shrugged. There was nothing to do now but go ahead with this. Andy
reached over and gave a good press to the old-
fashioned doorbell. They both heard it ring
inside and waited while footsteps approached
and the door opened.

They found themselves face-to-face with a
stern-looking woman in a plain gray dress and
starched white apron. It wasn't how either of
them had imagined Jane's mother.

"Hello, Mrs. Barrett," Toby said, taking
the lead. "We're Jane's roommates from
school."

"Mrs. Barrett is out at the moment with
Miss Jane. I am Bernice, the maid. I've instructions to ask you in and usher you to the
south parlor."

"*South* parlor?" Andy mouthed to Toby as
they followed Bernice through a large foyer
tiled in black and white squares. Overhead, a
huge crystal chandelier shimmered a soft light
on everything.

They continued down a wide hall until
they came to a pair of doors painted dove-
gray. Bernice pushed them open and, with a

quick flourish of her arm, indicated that Toby and Andy should go in.

"Miss Charlotte will see to you presently," Bernice said with no change in her dour expression. And then she backed out, closing the doors as she went.

The two roommates looked around.

"Reminds you of 407, doesn't it?" Andy said sarcastically. The room was beautiful and lavishly furnished, like something out of one of the decorating magazines her mother got. She recognized the style as Early American. The fireplace had a mantel of white painted wood. Above it was a gilded carving of an American eagle. Facing each other in front of the fireplace were matching sofas upholstered in a navy fabric with a print of tiny flowers. The floors were made of highly polished wood planks and scattered with thick Aubusson rugs.

"All the books are on sailing," Toby said, as she stood in front of the built-in mahogany bookcases.

"Oh, yes, sailing!" Andy said in a terrible Boston accent. "The very essence of life, don't you think?"

"Oh . . ." Toby said, catching on to the game, "well, of course. What *would* life be without starboard and mizzenmasts and regattas," she babbled on, pulling every nautical term she could out of her memory, as she flung herself in a debutante impersonation into a huge, dark, leather armchair in the corner. "Hey. What's this?" she said, pulling on a long velvet rope hanging down from the ceiling by the chair.

Andy shook her head and said, "Don't know."

"Toot toot!" Toby said, tugging on it as if she were a train engineer.

Almost immediately, the doors to the room were opened again, but in place of Bernice was a tall thin man in black trousers and a striped vest. Clearly the butler.

"You rang?" he said.

Toby looked at her hand on the rope and instantly got the picture.

"Ooops," was all she could say.

"The young ladies would perhaps like some tea?" he said.

"Oh, heavens, yes," Andy said, fooling around. "Tea! Of course. We simply must have our tea. And crumpets, of course."

"And scones," said Toby, who had no idea what scones were. But anytime she had ever read a book set in England, people were always having them with their tea.

"And cherries jubilee to finish off," Andy added. "That's what we always have at Canby Hall."

"Very good," the butler said, nodding and backing out of the room the same way Bernice had.

"You think he understood we were just kidding?" Toby asked Andy.

"Of course," Andy said, going over and moving a few pieces around on a chessboard set up on a table by the window. "Check and mate," she added.

"Maybe someone was in the middle of a game." Toby came over and inspected the game board.

"Oh, do you think so?" Andy gasped. "I thought it was just kind of sitting there, gathering dust. Here, I think I can remember how I moved the pieces. Let's see. I think this goes here and this was over here and this one, oh. . . . Help, Toby, I can't remember."

Just then the doors opened for a third time and an imposing young woman stood in the doorway. She was tall and slightly overweight and wore her blond hair in a rather severe pageboy. She was wearing a dark green dress. Her style was that of someone much older than she was.

"Hello," she said, not unfriendly, but not exactly brimming over with warmth, either. "I am Jane's sister, Charlotte. And I assume you are October and Andrea. I trust you had a pleasant trip in."

"Uh, oh, yes," Andy stammered. "It was a real, well, a real ride in a car." She didn't know what to say. Jane had always raved about her sister, Charlotte. How great she was. How smart. What a big help she always was in solving Jane's problems. With all that build-up, Andy had been expecting a different kind of person. Someone a little more with it. This young woman looked like somebody's stuffy aunt, not somebody's cool sister.

"I hope your stay at the Barrett house is equally pleasing," she said. "If you come with me now, I'll show you to your room."

Just then, there was a clanking sound that grew louder and louder until it suddenly stopped behind Charlotte in the doorway. There was an elaborate silver tea service set on a wheeled cart.

Charlotte turned, startled. "What is this, Walton?"

"Tea, Miss.'

"I don't recall ordering tea," she said, a little indignantly.

"The young ladies did, Miss," he said.

"Oh, I see," Charlotte said, then turned back to Andy and Toby and said, "I see you've made yourselves quite at home without my help." This statement had a heavy overlay of sarcasm to it.

"Oh, we didn't really mean to order all this," Toby said, trying to straighten things out. "We were just fooling around."

"Fooling around?" Charlotte said, arching an eyebrow, as if she had never heard of the term. Then she turned back to the butler and told him to please serve. "Just what do we have here?" she said, inspecting the cart as it rolled by her.

"Tea and scones and crumpets, Miss."

"Yes, Walton, but what on earth is that ghastly thing that seems to be on fire?"

"Cherries jubilee, Miss. The cook had to look it up special. But it was what the young ladies specifically asked for. Seems it's what they have every day at Miss Jane's school."

Charlotte looked incredulously down at the flaming cherries, then across the room at Toby and Andy.

"I'll leave you to your tea, then," she said tersely. "Walton will show you to your room when you're finished."

"Uh," Toby said, punting, "maybe you'd like to join us, Charlotte."

"Thank you, but I think not. We're having dinner in less than an hour, so a meal doesn't seem quite appropriate at the moment." And with that she left the room.

Toby and Andy watched as Walton the butler set their tea out on the low table between the sofas and then, when he'd left the room, they looked across the food and tea cups at each other with gloomy faces.

"Well," Andy said sarcastically, "looks like we're off to a great start here."

CHAPTER SEVEN

The little guest room where the butler put Andy and Toby was high up in the house, under the eaves.

"Oh, Andy," Toby sighed when they were left alone there. "I think this might be the nicest room I've ever seen."

Everything was painted white — the walls, the beams overhead, even the wood floors. The lace curtains at the small windows were white, as were the two iron bedsteads. The only smudges of color were the antique quilts on the two beds, each patchworked in pastel colors, faded with time.

Toby sat on the edge of one of the beds and looked around slowly. Suddenly her eyes began to water. Andy saw this, rushed over, and sat next to her friend.

"What's wrong? You didn't like your cherries jubilee?" she said, trying to kid Toby into a better mood.

Toby smiled a weak smile and shook her head.

"It's just that I've always dreamed of having a room like this, a comfy little place all my own. And fixed up like this — pretty but not fancy."

Andy looked around, appraising the room, then said, "Well, it's a nice little place for sure, but it doesn't exactly seem like The Impossible Dream."

"It sort of is if you live with your father, who's a great rancher and a terrific dad, but not too tuned into decorating. We've lived plain so long I wouldn't even know how to put together a nice room if I tried."

"Oh. Is that why you only have that ragtag old army blanket on your bed and nothing at all on your wall in 407? Why, you poor thing!"

Instead of cheering her up, Andy's sympathy had the reverse effect of making Toby *really* start to cry.

"Hey," Andy said, pulling a handkerchief out of her little shoulder purse and handing it over, "come on. Dry those tears. I promise as soon as we get back to school, I will personally offer my ever-so-tasteful, yet extremely avant-garde, decorating consultation. We can go around to the secondhand stores and see if we can pick up an old quilt like this. Maybe a little rug for next to your bed. Maybe a tea bag cozy."

"A what?"

Well, you know how the English have tea
cozies — knitted covers to keep their pots of
tea warm? Well, maybe you need a little
knitted cozy to keep that tea bag of yours
warm, while it hangs from the ceiling all
winter."

This brought a smile to Toby's face.

"Tobe," Andy pressed. "Are you ever going
to tell me what that tea bag's all about?"

Toby looked at Andy, and then, after a
moment, paused in thought, opened her mouth
to say something.

Just at that exact moment, though, the door
burst open and there was Jane.

"You guys! Well, so how do you like it so
far? Isn't Boston the ultimate?! And you've
got to admit that Louisburg Square is unique.
And I hear you already met Charlotte. Isn't
she the greatest sister in the world? Aren't you
going to get ready for dinner?"

These questions came in such a rapid-fire
barrage that Toby and Andy couldn't squeeze
in an answer to any but the last of them.

"Oh, we're ready," Toby said.

"As ready as we'll ever be," Andy added,
still feeling full from the scones and crumpets
and cherries jubilee, but not wanting to mention it.

"Oh yes, well . . ." Jane said, clearly having
trouble getting to the point. "You see, the
thing is we sort of dress for dinner here."

"Well, these are my best corduroys," Toby said.

"That's nice, Tobe," Jane said, as if she were speaking to a kindergartener. "But did you bring a dress? Oh no, that's right, you don't have a dress. What about a skirt?"

"I've got my denim one with me," Toby said, beginning to feel like a prize colt being brushed for display at the State Fair.

"Denim?" Jane said. "Well, I guess it'll have to do." Then she turned to Andy. "What about you?"

"What *about* me?" Andy said. She could get pretty indignant when the occasion called for it. "I am *already* wearing a skirt and a sweater."

"Well," Jane said. "You must admit it's not quite a sweater. A Tina Turner sweat shirt is not a sweater; am I right?" Jane was trying to keep a light cajoling tone in her voice. She didn't want to upset Andy, but she was dealing with other pressures.

"Look, you two. Please. Dressing up a bit for dinner is just how they do it around here. I personally don't care if you come down dressed in tutus and top hats. But Mother and Father will think you didn't care enough to make a nice start with them. They'll just think you're punks and they won't get to know how wonderful you really are and — "

"All right! Stop! We get the point," Andy

said, grabbing Jane by the shoulders and shaking her gently.

"Oh," Jane said, calming down. "Okay."

"We'll put on our gowns and tiaras and be downstairs in ten minutes," Andy said.

"Do you think I should leave the velvet train on my dress? Or do you think that would be just a little too much?" Toby asked, with such an air of innocence that all of them had to crack up at the image.

"Oh, you two are so great!" Jane said, giving them both big hugs. "I know this isn't exactly your style. And I really appreciate you being such good sports about it. Now I've got to run and get ready myself."

"Hey!" Andy called after her. "What's for dinner?"

"Oh, I don't know, something simple probably," Jane said, sticking her head back in for a moment, then rushing off.

"Macaroni and cheese, probably," Toby said as she got her skirt out of the duffel. "That's what me and my Dad usually have on Friday nights."

"Uh, I don't know, Tobe," Andy said. "For some reason I don't think the Barretts *ever* eat mac and cheese."

When Toby and Andy got downstairs, they followed the sounds of talk and laughter until they found the dining room, its doors thrown open and the Barrett family inside, seated around a table large enough to accommodate a couple of football teams.

As soon as Jane saw them, she rushed up and made introductions between her roommates and her parents.

"And Charlotte, of course, you've already met."

Charlotte nodded at them in a vague, distracted way, as though they'd come to fix the furnace and were just passing through on their way to the basement. Jane's mother, though, clapped her hands in delight.

"Girls! How nice to meet you at last! Jane has told us so much about both of you." She was tall and stately. She had blond hair like her daughters, but wore it up in a formal, kind of old-fashioned style. She was wearing a simple black cocktail dress with a short strand of pearls. Toby took one look at Mrs. Barrett and the fine silver and crystal and patterned china on the white linen tablecloth and felt like she was an interplanetary visitor — totally out of place.

Jane's father was already sitting at the head of the table. To Andy, he looked like the typical businessman in ads for credit cards and first-class air travel. He had a broad face and wore a navy pinstripe suit, thin-rimmed tortoiseshell glasses, and a thin gold watch. As the girls came into the dining room, he was signing some papers with a heavy black and gold fountain pen.

He looked up amid the flurry of introductions and said, "Sorry, girls. Rude of me to be doing business at the table, I know. But there's a messenger in the hall waiting for these. I won't be a minute."

"Do come in and sit down," Mrs. Barrett said, gesturing toward their chairs as Walton pulled them out.

"There," Mr. Barrett said, sliding the papers into a large envelope and handing them to Walton. Then he pulled his napkin off the table, spread it across his lap, and looked down the length of the table at Andy and Toby.

"So," he said, "I hear we have representatives here at the table tonight from the Windy City and the Lone Star State."

Andy groaned to herself. Mr. Barrett was going to be — no doubt about it — one of the worst types of parent. The Corny Father. Corny fathers were all the same. They started off with statements like this one — to which there was no possible answer. And then when the poor teenager didn't respond, the Corny Father usually asked something maddening like "Cat got your tongue?"

"Cat got your tongue?" Mr. Barrett asked now.

Argh, Andy thought.

"Now, now, David," Mrs. Barrett said. "Don't tease the girls so much. They may not understand yet what a wit you are." And then she turned to Bernice and said, "Will you bring the first course in? I think we're all ready to eat."

In what seemed like a split second, Bernice was back, placing in front of them a plate with the first course on it.

Toby kicked Andy under the table and muttered out of the side of her mouth, "What in tarnation is it? Boiled pine cone?"

"Artichokes," Andy muttered from behind her napkin, but there was no way she could explain to Toby fast enough how to eat it.

"You don't like artichokes, Toby?" Mrs. Barrett asked, arching a curious eyebrow.

"Oh no, ma'am, I just love 'em," Toby said, faking as much enthusiasm as she could. Then, to back up this statement, she picked hers up and took a good-sized bite out of it.

Her face went into contortions as she tried to chew on what tasted like a mouthful of leaves. As she was working her way through this mouthful, she happened to look across the table and saw Charlotte, who was eating *her* artichoke by pulling off each leaf, dipping it into a little pool of sauce to the side of the plate, then scraping the leaves with her teeth as she pulled them out of her mouth and placing them neatly around the rim of the plate.

"Oh, I see you eat them Boston-style," Toby said weakly, after she was finally able to swallow.

The nightmare only got worse as further

courses were brought out. Andy's knit tie flipped into her cup of Boston clam chowder. Worse, she was talking and didn't see it for a while. Long enough for the soup to soak half-way up the tie before she noticed it.

And then came the soft-shell crabs. First Toby tried to graciously take the whole platter from the maid, thinking that passing it down the table was what was expected of her, only to have Mrs. Barrett say in a crisp tone, "No, my dear. Those are for everyone. There aren't enough for you to have them all. Just take what you want and let Bernice serve the others."

Then, trying to work her way out of this humiliation, Toby tried to eat the funny little crabs in the most mannerly way she could think of — cutting away ever so delicately, peeling little bits of shell off as she went, until Mrs. Barrett finally interjected, "No, dear. You just eat the whole thing, shell and all."

And then after the crab, came the little bowls with water and lemon wedges in them. Jane had mentioned something about a "pal-ate refresher" between courses; Toby assumed this was it, and drank hers. As soon as she was done, she saw everyone else washing their fingers in theirs, and knew she'd made yet an-other miserable error. The "palate refresher" turned out to be some fruit sherbet. Why didn't they just call things what they were?

Toby wondered, burning with embarrassment and rage from the whole humiliating meal.

All the while they were flunking this pop quiz on Weird Foods of the Rich and Famous, the girls were also having to make conversation with the Barretts, which was also no mean feat.

Mr. Barrett had picked up on Toby's line about eating artichokes "Boston-style," and whenever she did something stupid, which seemed to her like about every other minute, he would point it out in a joking way, like, "And here we use our finger bowls Boston-style," he would say, dunking his fingers in and out exaggeratedly, and then laughing heartily. As if this were going to strike her as really funny and make her feel terrific.

"What've we got here? A lead balloon?" he'd say then, in response to Toby's mortified expression.

As corny as Mr. Barrett was, Toby found him easier to take than Mrs. Barrett, who helpfully offered little corrections every time Toby goofed.

But the worst person at the table, as far as either of them was concerned, was Charlotte, who maintained a silence throughout the whole meal that was like a high stone wall. They were both sure that behind it, she was laughing up her sleeve at the hicks from the sticks.

Each had her own separate, private thoughts on Charlotte. Andy thought, You snobby rich girl sitting over there looking down your nose at me. Well, I'll just show you. And worse thoughts than that.

Toby just thought, Grrrrr.

By the end of dinner, Toby was exhausted from lurching between being mortified at her latest foul-up to worrying what her next one was going to be. She was incredibly relieved when dessert turned out to be just pie, a recognizable food item that she could eat "Boston-style" as well as anyone else.

Neither of them could have pushed through the meal if they hadn't been doing it for Jane. The more mistakes they made, the worse they felt, but the more they thought they had to press on and try to save the evening for her. It would have been awful to abandon her when she was working so hard at getting her family to like them.

"Mother, you know Andrea is terribly interested in the ballet," Jane said at one point, in a much more refined tone of voice than she used around Baker House. "She's a wonderful dancer."

"Is that right?" Mrs. Barrett replied. "Then we'll have to try to get you together with Misha next time he's in town."

"Misha?" Andy said.

"Mikhail Baryshnikov," Mrs. Barrett said.

"He's another wonderful dancer who's a friend of the family."

Andy gulped. In her opinion, Baryshnikov was the world's greatest ballet dancer. In her wildest dreams she couldn't imagine meeting him. And she would absolutely die if Mrs. Barrett introduced him to her as "another wonderful dancer who's a friend of the family." She was clearly way out of her depth around here. Luckily, Mrs. Barrett had by now turned her attentions to Toby.

"Jane tells me you live on a ranch. That must be fascinating, living in such a wild and primitive place. Do they still have cattle drives and shoot rustlers?"

Toby grimaced behind her grin. Sometimes she couldn't believe the things people actually said about Texas. The ones who didn't think everybody in the state was a gunfighter watched *Dallas* and thought all Texans were millionaires. She knew Mrs. Barrett was just trying to be polite. But she was also pretty sure that under the politeness, Jane's mother thought Toby had been raised by wolves. She probably had her doubts about Andy, too, after she'd dipped her tie in the soup.

You had to give Andy points for trying, though. Now she was rising above her embarrassment and nervousness to start up a little conversation with the Barretts.

"We're really looking forward to the party tomorrow night," she lied sweetly.

"Well, good. I'm glad to hear it," Mrs. Barrett said, then added, "And if you have any questions about how anything is done, just ask Jane."

"She thinks we're going to come in our bathrobes and square dance," Andy whispered to Toby, who nodded. Out of the corner of her eye, she was pretty sure she saw Charlotte cover a smirk with her linen napkin.

Finally, after nearly two hours of captivity at the Barretts' dining room table, the warden released them.

"Jane," Mr. Barrett said, "why don't you give the girls the grand tour of the house?"

"Okay, Father," Jane said.

"I myself am going to put my next move on the telex to Olaf. I think I've come up with a brilliant strategy. I want to see what Olaf makes of it."

Jane turned to her roommates and explained.

"Father has been playing this chess game with a guy in Norway for nearly two years. They make their moves by telex. I think the family takes a second place in Father's heart. I'm pretty sure that chess game is the thing he most looks forward to every night when he gets home."

"Uh oh," Toby said through clenched jaws. Andy just gulped.

CHAPTER EIGHT

Late that night, up in the little room in the attic, Andy and Toby were lying snug under their quilts looking out the windows at the moonlight filtering through a snowy sky. They had been silent for a long time before Andy finally said what was on both their minds.

"I just thought of a great title for a horror movie. *Dinner of the Living Dead*."

"I know," Toby groaned. "I can't believe I just grabbed that artichokey thing and bit into it like it was an old plug of chewing tobacco. Then, slurping up that finger bowl!"

"You? At least you didn't soak up your entire cup of soup with your tie. Of course, that's how we do it, Chicago-style."

This started them giggling, and they couldn't stop for quite a while. When they finally did, they both felt a little better.

"We should stop torturing ourselves about

our performance," Andy said, trying to get back some of her usual confidence. "After all, those Barretts weren't exactly giving us a whole lot of help."

"I know," Toby said. "It's hard to say who was the toughest one to deal with — Mrs. Barrett with her helpful little suggestions, or Mr. Barrett with all that corny kidding around. I thought I'd die. Of course I think I'll die of embarrassment about five times a day. I think I may be the most easily embarrassed person in the world. And then what about old Charlotte giving us the fish eye across the table? Oh, I don't care *what* they think of me."

"But you've got to, on account of Jane."

"Shh. Wait," Toby whispered. "Did you hear something?"

They were both still for a moment and heard a soft tap-tap-tapping, then the creak of the door being pushed open.

"You guys still awake?" came Jane's voice, calling in softly.

"Hey," Andy said, "come on in. We were just talking about you."

"Oh?" Jane teased, hopping onto Andy's bed and getting her into a fake stranglehold. "And just what were you saying behind my back?"

Andy pretended to gargle her words out.

"Just . . . just that we hoped we hadn't disgraced you too much in front of your family."

"Oh, don't worry about it," Jane said, then

sighed, flopped over onto her back, and dangled her head over the side of the bed, so that she was staring up at the ceiling, her long blond hair shimmering in the moonlight. "At least you were trying. I should've briefed you on the dinner. You got thrown a few curves with all that fancy food, I'm afraid. You were really sweet about it. I think Mother and Father liked you."

"What about your sister?" asked Toby, always frank to a fault. "She kept looking across the table at me as if she were trying to remember if she'd seen my face on a Wanted poster somewhere."

"I'm not sure what's going on with Charlotte," Jane said. "She's usually a little reserved — I think it has to do with being self-conscious about her weight — but not *that* reserved. She's even aloof from me this visit. It's like she's off somewhere else. But I don't know where. She was even worse with Cary."

"Oh," Andy said excitedly, "I was so absorbed in my own worries I forgot Cary was stopping by to meet your parents. How did that go?"

Jane sat up and leaned back against the iron footboard of the bed.

"Well," she said, "let's put it this way. You two were like Jackie Onassis and Princess Di compared to Cary's performance. He marched in doing his Sean Penn *Bad Boys* number. I think it's difficult for my parents to get into talking seriously to someone sitting in their drawing room wearing sunglasses and an earring and asking if there are any leftovers from dinner."

"He didn't?" Toby said, incredulous.

"Of course he did," Jane replied. "Why are you surprised? Being Cary, that's what he had to do. And that wasn't the worst of it. The worst was when he pulled out his little spiral notebook and told them he was 'doing' this party as a research project on the Boston ritual of ancestor worship."

"Your parents must've loved that," Andy said.

"I think my father thought he was joking. Mother took him seriously, though. She sat there with this kind of stunned look on her face. People don't usually say things like that around her. She didn't say anything about him to me after he left, which is a bad sign."

"Boy," Toby said, and let out a low whistle. "Just what you needed after that dinner."

"Well, at least it wasn't as *long* as dinner. Cary was meeting some old friends to go out to some rock clubs, and so he only stayed about twenty minutes."

"You didn't go out with him?" Toby said.

"No. I wanted to help Mother with the hats."

Andy and Toby, sensing something terrible underlying this statement, both sat up and simultaneously said, "*What* hats?"

"Oh," Jane said, "surely I told you. We're making each male guest at the party a little Pilgrim hat, each woman a bonnet. Each one is personalized. For instance, your bonnet, Toby, has a little horse on it. Andy, yours has a tiny ballet dancer pinned to the edge."

Toby and Andy looked at Jane in stunned disbelief.

"You've got to be kidding," Andy said.

"Pilgrim bonnet?" Toby said. "Sorry. No way."

Jane jumped off the bed and stormed over to the windows, where she stood looking out for a long moment, her back to them. She was either trying to cool off, or gathering her forces. They couldn't tell which.

Suddenly she wheeled around and lashed out at them. "You are so incredibly selfish! I'm fed up with all of you. Cary shows up looking like Keith Richards and you two display the table manners of cave dwellers. And now you're balking at the honor of wearing Pilgrim bonnets to the Barretts' Landing party?! Sometimes I think that with friends like you . . . well, as they say, who needs enemies?"

And with that she tore past them and out of the room. They sat in silence listening to her race down the hallway toward the stairs.

"Oh boy!" Andy sighed after a long moment. "And she hasn't even found out yet what I did to her father's chess game!"

CHAPTER
NINE

Toby awoke to a firm knocking on the door of the guest room. She blinked and grabbed her watch off the night table. Nine-fifteen.

She got up and tiptoed past Andy, who was still sound asleep. She opened the door to find Bernice the maid with a wicker tray of coffee and croissants, and a phone message.

It read: "Let's do Boston! Call me. Cary."

Which she did immediately from the phone on the night table. While she punched the numbers, she lifted the pillow Andy had put over her head. "Come on, sleepyhead. Time to get up." And then she said into the receiver, "Cary?"

"Hey!" he responded. "Do we have a date today for thrills and chills in Beantown? Or are you two Rip Van Winkles going to snooze the day away?"

"Oh no, we *definitely* want to go," she said.

"And I think the sooner we get out from under the Barretts' feet, the better."

"Why?" he asked. "Have you two joined the ranks of the riffraff, too?"

"Looks like it," Toby said. "We did about everything possible wrong last night, short of putting ketchup on Mr. Barrett's dinner jacket and eating it."

"I think I may have been a bit too much for them, too," he said. "I don't believe the Barretts are into the *Miami Vice* look. I think they just thought I forgot to shave and iron my clothes."

"I get the picture," Toby said, then asked him, "How soon can you get here?

"Half an hour?"

"Great. I'll roust Andy out of the sack. We'll meet you in front of the house. Maybe if we all get out of their hair for the day, they'll forget yesterday and we can make a fresh impression at the party tonight."

And so the three of them headed off into the heart of the city.

"First stop, Faneuil Hall and Quincy Market!" Cary shouted over the Talking Heads tape on the stereo.

"What's Quincy Market?" Andy shouted back.

"Only the most fun place in the whole city!" Cary said, grinning. "You'll see."

When they got there, the girls saw what he

meant. The markets were rows and rows of wonderful tiny shops and restaurants set along cobblestone malls.

"In the old old days, these were the fruit and vegetable markets," he explained. "Then they went to rack and ruin and were abandoned for a long time. About ten years ago, they spruced them up and reopened them with funky shops in the old stalls. Makes you wonder what everybody in Boston did on Sunday afternoon before then. Now they all come here."

"Oh look!" Toby exclaimed. "A whole shop devoted to rainbow stuff. I just love rainbows!"

"Come on, then!" Andy encouraged her. "Maybe we've found a decorating scheme for you."

Inside the shop, Toby immediately found the exactly perfect things — a rainbow print bedspread and matching throw rug.

"And oh, look!" she exclaimed, rushing across the shop and pointing upward. "A mobile of rainbows! To keep my tea bag company on the ceiling," she added with a sly grin.

Up at the register, Toby pulled out the credit card her father had given her for emergencies only.

"I'll have to call him before the bill comes in and explain what 'emergency' happened at someplace called The Rainbow Shop. I think he'll let me take this as an advance on my summer job money."

Cary was browsing around, being his usual sarcastic self, asking The Rainbow Shop saleswoman if she had "something in black and white." But after a while, even he got into the spirit of the place and bought Jane a satin pillow in the shape and colors of a rainbow.

"A little present probably isn't a bad idea," he said. "After my Academy Award-winning performance last night."

For the next hour or so, the three of them poked through the rows and rows of shops. Andy bought a chocolate bar in the shape of a ballet slipper. Cary found a Dire Straits pin to wear on his jeans jacket.

"Hey, you guys," Toby said as they were passing a popcorn shop, "I don't know about you, but I'm getting really hungry. Maybe we should go in here."

"Wait," Cary said, putting a restraining hand on her arm. "Don't waste your appetite on mere popcorn. There's a place down the way that serves real English fish and chips."

"What are fish and chips, anyway?" Toby wondered. "I've always read about them in English novels."

"They're really good," Cary assured her. "Large pieces of fish with a crisp coating. And the chips are really fries. And the Englishy thing about them is they're all wrapped up in waxed paper and you shake vinegar all over them from a bottle."

"Vinegar?!" Toby said, and made a puckered face.

"Don't knock it till you've tried it," Cary said, and swooped between the two girls and marched them straight over to the Union Jack Café.

"I'll try it, but I won't like it," Toby muttered as they went.

"Mmmm, good," Andy said, fifteen minutes later.

Toby just nodded *her* approval as her mouth was stuffed with fish and chips. As soon as she could speak, she said, "More vinegar, please."

Which cracked up all three of them.

When they were done eating, they piled back into Cary's car, punched a Duran Duran tape into the deck, and headed out on a winding tour of the city.

"There's the oldest restaurant in America," Cary said, pointing to an old building set on a curve. It was fronted with small-paned windows. "The Union Oyster House. We could've had lunch there."

"Don't push your luck," Toby said. "The fish and chips were great, but there's no way I'd go near an oyster."

Andy shook her head and said to Cary, "The

girl eats every day at Canby Hall and then turns up her nose at an oyster. Don't ask me to explain."

"Is the food at Canby Hall as bad as the food at Oakley Prep?" he wondered.

"Oh, I think no matter how bad yours is, ours has got to be worse," Andy said.

"Yeah," Toby added. "The other day Dee — she works breakfasts in the dining hall — said that in the back of the kitchen, by the loading dock, there's a whole bunch of big cartons. Government surplus or something. They're marked 'Grade E — Edible.' "

"You've got to be making that up," Cary said.

Toby shook her head no, then looked out the window. "What's that?" she asked, pointing out at a glass skyscraper.

"The John Hancock Tower," Cary told her, and then drove them by several of his favorite landmarks.

"What a cute little house!" Andy exclaimed, when Cary had pulled up to the curb in front of an old-fashioned clapboard house with gables and windows leaded into diamond shapes.

"Paul Revere lived here," he said.

"The British are coming! The British are coming!" Andy shouted.

"Get them some fish and chips!" Toby shouted.

Cary laughed, then got a sudden idea.

"Hey," he said. "Why don't we go to the

Smyth Museum? That's where Jane's family's collection is. Her mother's the curator, you know."

"Great idea," Andy said. "It'll give us something to talk about with Mrs. B. The family collection. Hmmm. I suppose I could tell her about *my* family's collection."

"What's that?" Cary asked.

"Fortune cookie fortunes. Whenever any of us goes out to a Chinese restaurant, we always bring back our fortune, put our initial on it, and pin it up on the bulletin board in the family room. And then we see what comes true."

"How's it going?" he aked.

"Well, lately it seems I'm living my mother's life. All her fortunes keep coming true for me."

The Smyth Museum was located on Beacon Hill, in a gray stone building that looked like a Greek temple. On the way in, the guard looked askance at Cary in his green leather jacket and beat-up black Levi's and his ever-present sunglasses.

"It's all right," Cary told the guard, "I'm not an international art thief — just a punk."

"Smart aleck," Toby teased Cary when they had gone a few feet farther. He just smiled, taking this as a compliment.

Toby and Andy were both getting to know Cary a lot better as the day went on. In the ladies' room, they had a chance to compare notes on their opinions of him.

"He's really kind of neat in his own weird way, don't you think?" Andy said.

"Oh yeah," Toby said. "I really like him. And I think he's good for Jane. She can't get too stuffy with *him* around."

"Right," Andy agreed. "Definitely a case of opposites attracting. Not like her and Neal. He's *way* too stuffy."

"You think so?" said Toby, who had gotten to know Neal better during the time Jane had been breaking up with him. "I think he's just been trapped into being that way by his family and his social set. I think there's a wild mountain lion inside him, trying to break free."

Andy, who had been combing her hair in the mirror next to Toby, turned to look at her friend in amazement. Clearly things had progressed between Toby and Neal, and quite a bit further than she had known. Mountain lion. Hmmm.

When they met Cary again in the lobby of the museum, he bowed from the waist; said, "This way, ladies"; and ushered them along a long corridor until they stood in front of a high archway.

Above it, a brass plaque read: THE BARRETT AMERICAN COLLECTION.

"Wow," Toby said, truly impressed.

"Well, I'll be," said Andy.

There was a desk just past the entrance, with a woman sitting behind it.

"Welcome to the Barrett Collection," she said to them. "Perhaps you'd like to take some literature on the collection and the family." She indicated with a wave of her hand several stacks of brochures lined up on the edge of the desk. Andy picked up the pamphlet on the Barrett family and flipped through it. After a moment, she gave out a low whistle.

"It's all true," she said. "Everything Jane's been telling us about her family."

"Did you think she was lying?" Cary asked.

"Oh no," Andy said quickly. "Of course not. It's just that, well . . . we really love Jane, you know, but she has a way of talking about her family that comes off kind of like bragging. Seeing it here in print and pictures, well, it just looks like plain fact that her family is really important around here."

Toby, meanwhile, had ventured off a ways and was looking at some of the paintings and sculpture in the collection. She turned to Cary and Andy and said, "Yeah, the only problem is that knowing how important the Barretts are only makes me more nervous about their party tonight."

"Don't worry," Cary said, trying to sound reassuring. "Remember, this is a party where all the guests are going to be wearing Pilgrim hats. So everybody is going to seem at least a little odd. So maybe we won't stand out all that much. Come on, we've got art to look at here."

They spent an hour or so looking at the collection, and wound up impressed with the selection of American art put together by the Barrett family, especially the contemporary work that had been bought by Jane's mother.

When they were on their way out, Cary said, "Well, now that we've soaked up a little culture, why don't we do something with absolutely no artistic or intellectual merit?"

"All *right*," Andy said, slapping his palm. "Clothes shopping!"

"You are really sensitive," Toby told him. "Knowing just what we want to do."

"Well, actually," he admitted, "what I meant was going to this great video game parlor I know. But if the purchase of wearable garments is what your female souls crave, I think I know just the place. My sister says Filene's basement is the world's single greatest site of bargains galore."

"Then what are we waiting for?!" Andy asked.

"But what will *you* do while we shop?" Toby asked Cary.

"Oh, I'll tag along. Keep you from putting your parents' charge cards into orbit. I'll serve as your fashion consultant. All the celebrities have them!"

* * *

Filene's turned out to be an old, established department store. Filene's basement, on the other hand, was a madhouse, an asylum for shoppers gone insane. Women stood elbow-to-elbow at every rack of marked-down merchandise. Andy and Toby saw a woman take off her own coat to try on a sweater. The woman standing next to her turned and eyed the coat with interest and got it half on before the owner noticed and shouted, "Hey, wait a minute! That's *my* coat you've got there!"

This struck the girls as extremely funny. They got into the wacky spirit of the place right away and started scouring the racks themselves.

Cary was as big a help as he had promised. First he talked Toby out of a red sweater that had been marked down three times.

"You've got all the red you need on top of your head," he said, rumpling her curls. And then he persuaded Andy to buy a seventy-five-percent-off silk shirt in an extremely weird print.

"Go for it," he said. "Who knows? You might fall in love with some weird guy the way Jane fell for me. And this way you'll already have something weird to wear on your first date."

To show him their appreciation for bringing them there, the girls bought Cary a unisex tie in the shape of a fish.

"We'll get you some chips to go with it," Toby teased.

When they came up out of the basement, they were all ravenous again and headed up the street for a pizza-by-the-slice place.

"I'd better call Jane," Andy said, when they'd gotten a table. "Let her know we're on our way back."

She went to the pay phone in the back and dialed the Barrett house. The butler answered and told her, "Miss Jane is extremely anxious to speak with you."

As it turned out, "anxious" wasn't quite the right word. When Jane finally got on the line, she shouted, "Just where are you?!"

"I don't know," Andy said. "Some pizza joint by Filene's. You've got to hear what a crazy, wonderful day we've had."

"What I want to hear," Jane said, her voice cold as stone, "is just where you've been and why you didn't even tell me you were leaving the house this morning."

"Jane. We just didn't want to wake you up. You knew Cary was taking us on a tour of the city. It was you who arranged it."

"I don't remember that."

"You're too preoccupied to remember. But we *did* think you knew where we were today. And you've got to believe that or else you'll have to think we're pretty rotten, insensitive roommates. Which we are not."

"I thought you were upset after last night," Jane said. "After I yelled at you and ran out of the room." Andy could hear her sniffling a little on the other end of the line, and so knew Jane was mostly hurt rather than mad.

"Jane. In 407, someone's shouting and running out of the room practically every other day. Do you think we'd let a little thing like that send us packing?"

"I guess not," Jane said, following with more sniffles.

"We'll be there right away," Andy said.

"Hurry up, though. The party's only two hours off. And plus, well . . . I miss you guys. My family gets pretty nervous in the crunch right before the party. It's pretty hairy around here at the moment."

"Maybe we can tell them a few jokes. Lighten them up," Andy suggested.

"Oh, I don't think so. You guys are one of the biggest sore points around here at the moment. Mother and Father and Charlotte think you just disappeared today to avoid having to help with the party. They pretty much think you're the lowest of the low."

"Oh good, Jane," Andy said sarcastically. "That's great. That makes me feel really relaxed, knowing we'll be coming back into such a warm and loving situation. Do you think you could tell them that it was all a misunderstanding, that we were only trying to get out from underfoot, not to duck work?"

"Things are just so majorly hectic around here at the moment. But if I can get anyone's attention, I'll be sure to mention it," Jane said.

Andy hung up and went back to the table where Cary and Toby were happily munching away at their pizza. She gave them the details of her conversation with Jane.

"And so, if Jane gets around to telling her family that we're not thoughtless and selfish, this should be a lovely evening."

"If they're pointing muskets out the windows when we get there," Cary said, wiping pizza sauce off his chin with a paper napkin, "I'll drop you around the block."

Toby and Andy laughed, but inside, both of them were still worried about the reception awaiting them on Louisburg Square.

CHAPTER TEN

When they got back to Jane's, she was waiting for them and opened the door. Inside, the house was buzzing with activity. Florist delivery people were dashing in with huge ceramic urns full of red and white roses. The cook was bellowing from the kitchen, clearly furious with Bernice for letting some sauce boil over. Extra maids and waiters were setting up the buffet table and champagne bar. Two men in gray jumpsuits were giving the wood floors a last-minute glow with huge electric buffers. Tuxedoed members of the band were beginning to file in with their instruments.

"Can you believe that in a couple of hours all this chaos will somehow turn into a party?" Jane said, throwing her hands up in the air. "So tell me what fun you guys had all day while I was slaving away making centerpieces for the buffet table."

They gave her a brief summary of the highlights and promised to tell her all the details later, after the party. She kissed Cary good-bye and sent him off to change for the party.

In the midst of this chaos, Mrs. Barrett was high on a stepladder looping red, white, and blue crepe paper out from the crystal chandelier in the front hall. Through open doors, the girls could see Mr. Barrett on the phone in the south parlor, shouting so loudly he had to be on long *long* distance.

"No!" he was yelling, "I distinctly remember my last move was my knight to your bishop."

Andy nudged Toby and crossed her eyes at her — their private signal for "eek!"

"Come on upstairs and see my dress for the party," Jane said, taking their hands and rushing up the red-carpeted stairs to the second floor.

When they got to her room — a wonderfully light and airy place with lilac-patterned wallpaper and a canopy bed — she ran to the closet and pulled out her dress.

"See?" she said. "Isn't it gorgeous?" And it was. Pink tulle with a swooshing skirt, and strapless. A dancing dress. Toby and Andy were both envious. Neither of them had brought along *anything* like this.

"Jane, dear," came a voice from the hallway. It was Charlotte, in a blue robe, and hot rollers. "Do you have some blush I could borrow?" she asked. Then, noticing that Andy and Toby were in the room, she gave them an almost invisible nod and said, "Oh. Hello, girls."

"Here," Jane said, and gave her a bottle of blush off the top of her dresser. "You're so much closer to ready than I am, Char. Do you have a date for the party? One of your friends from Harvard?"

Charlotte seemed to grow flustered at this question.

"Oh, uh, no. I didn't want a date for this party. Actually, I don't want to have to worry about someone else's good time tonight. I want to be free to help Mother and Father if they need me."

This sounded pretty phony to Toby, but she didn't say anything.

"Hey," Andy filled in the pause, "we'd better get ready ourselves. Come on, Tobe." And the two of them raced up the back stairs to their attic hideaway. When they got there, they flopped onto their beds.

Andy grew pensive, then after a little while asked Toby, "Do you think Charlotte hates us, or what?"

"I don't know," Toby said. "At first I thought she was this big snob, but now I'm not so sure. She seems kind of on auto pilot, even with Jane, and she can't be snobby about her own sister. They have the same blue blood

or whatever they think it is. I think maybe
she's got a problem."

"A secret tragic romance," Andy said.

"Oh Andy. You're always seeing secret ro-
mances around every corner."

"And I'm usually right, I might add. Do not
forget, girl, that I was the first one at Canby
Hall to discern that Alison was out of love
with Michael Frank and on her way to marry-
ing David Gordon."

"All right, all right, so you get a lucky guess
now and then," Toby said.

"Lucky guess, my foot," Andy said.

"Hey," Toby said. "Forget about Charlotte
for a second and help me worry about how
my outfit is probably not nearly good enough
for this party."

"I was just thinking the same thing about
mine. Seeing Jane's dress gave me the sinking
knowledge that mine is majorly tacky compared to it." She sprung from the bed and
pulled it from the closet.

"Oh, it's fine," Toby said, meaning this sincerely. She liked Andy's taste in clothes and
thought the red miniskirt and white top that
Andy was holding up were great. "And it's
nice and unwrinkly. You were smart to think
of hanging it up when we got here. My stuff
is still in my suitcase. Probably as crushed as
tinfoil around a sandwich in the bottom of a
lunchbag."

"Oh Tobe, how could you just leave it all scrunched up in your luggage? We'd better get it out right away."

They pulled it from her duffel. What they found had at one time been a pretty nice brown skirt with a blue shirt and tan vest. Now, though, what Toby held in her hands was three clumps of wrinkled cloth. The outfit looked as though it had been put through a trash masher and survived, but just barely.

"Oh no!" Toby exclaimed. "What am I going to do?"

"Quick," Andy said. "Go turn the shower full blast on hot and we'll give it the old steam method. Don't worry. It's tried and true."

Ten minutes later, both of them were standing in the bathroom off their room, dripping with sweat, their hair completely frizzled. The skirt and top, however, hanging from the shower rod, were as wrinkled as ever.

"Tried and true, eh?" Toby said dismally.

"Well, it's *true* I hadn't *tried* it on this outfit," Andy admitted. "I guess there's nothing left but to press it. We'll simply have to find an iron."

"Where are we going to find an iron and ironing board half an hour before the biggest party in Boston, with all the Barretts running around like mad dogs?"

"Come on, we're wily," Andy prompted, giving Toby a hand up from her bed. "Let's go down those back stairs. They probably lead to servants' rooms, and where there are servants, there's probably an ironing board. Really, sometimes I think I'd make an absolutely brilliant detective."

In response to this, Toby gave Andy a shove out of the room.

The back stairs, unlike the wide, carpeted front ones, were narrow and wooden and creaky.

"Sssh," Andy said, turning back when they'd gone down half a flight and hit a really groaning board. "We don't want anyone to see us skulking around like this."

At the bottom of the short flight, the stairs abruptly went down off to the side.

"This is odd," Andy said. "Did you ever see a staircase that took a right angle like this?"

Toby came up behind Andy and briefly lost her footing. She fell against the wall to their left, and all of a sudden it made a tiny clicking sound and sprung open slightly, like a door. Toby gasped.

"Oh wow!" Andy breathed. "It looks like we've stumbled onto a secret passage. I thought they only existed in mystery stories."

"We probably shouldn't go in," Toby said.

"Oh right," Andy replied sarcastically. "Let's just forget the boring old secret passage and take the regular stairs. I'm a little tired of secret passages this month, anyway."

Toby grinned sheepishly, pushed the wall/

door open a little further, and peered in. "It's pitch-black in here," she said.

"Reach around and see if you can find a light switch," Andy suggested. But after a minute or so of trying, Toby shook her head. "No luck. I'll go get my flashlight."

Andy looked at her incredulously.

"You carry a flashlight? Along with your change purse and lipstick?"

"Well, when you live on a ranch, you learn to carry one all the time. It can get pretty dark out on the range at night. I guess old habits die hard."

"And am I *glad* in this case," Andy admitted.

Toby ran to fetch the flashlight and was back in a minute. She and Andy stood looking at each other for a moment before Toby finally said, "Okay, let's go."

She pulled open the wall/door as far as it would go — just far enough for them to slip in sideways. Inside, it was dark and stuffy and eerily silent.

"Look," Toby said, aiming her flashlight downward. "A secret stairway."

"Maybe we should just skip this after all," Andy said nervously.

Toby had to laugh. "Now look who's chicken," she teased.

"Okay. Okay. Let's go down," Andy said. "The worst we could find would be a trap door over a pit of alligators."

"Alligators?!" Toby shouted.

"Sssh," Andy said. "Just kidding."

"Oh Andy. This place is scary enough without you putting monsters in my mind. Come on and follow me — and no more jokes or tricks." She took Andy's hand and the two of them took each creaky step slowly, together.

The stairs wound around and went down what seemed to be about three flights. There was no exit anywhere along the way. Suddenly, Toby turned to Andy and asked, "Are you wearing perfume?"

"No. Why?"

"Don't you smell it? All the way down. Like lilacs."

Andy sniffed. "Yeah, now that you mention it. What do you think it is?"

"Maybe someone who wears lilac perfume uses this passage."

"But who?"

"I don't know," Toby said. "Maybe we'll find out."

Finally they reached the bottom.

"It's a dead end," Andy said over Toby's shoulder. They were looking at a blank wall.

"No," Toby said pensively, "stairs *always* go somewhere. They never just go nowhere. Let's try the same trick we accidentally tried at the top. Let's just push this wall here."

But nothing happened.

"We didn't exactly push it," Andy said.

"Remember, you sort of fell against it. Try that again."

And so Toby backed up and came down the final few steps again and at the last minute, thudded her whole body into the wall to her left. And sure enough, it clicked open just like the one at the top.

"Atta girl," Andy said, clapping Toby on the shoulder, then pulling the spring door open enough so they could get through.

Immediately, they were in the middle of hanging clothes, tripping over a floor full of shoes.

"We're in a closet," Toby whispered. "And that lilac smell is stronger than ever."

"Shhh," Toby said, putting her hand over Andy's mouth. "What're those sounds? Voices?"

Andy pried Toby's hand off and whispered, "The alligators."

This cracked them both up. They started laughing so hard, and then trying to not laugh, and then trying to stop each other from laughing, that they wound up hanging on to each other and finally losing their balance and falling against the front door to the closet and out into the room beyond.

It was a basement servants' lounge. In it was McNulty, the Barretts' chauffeur, a small, thin young man with thick glasses. The girls knew him by sight from the times he drove Jane back to school after weekends at home.

What they didn't know was that he and Charlotte Barrett were romantically involved. At least that's how it looked, given that at the particular moment Andy and Toby fell into the lounge, he and Charlotte were kissing.

They really made an odd couple. Charlotte stood nearly a head taller than McNulty. (She must call him something else, Toby thought. She couldn't call him McNulty.) She also outweighed him by quite a few pounds. Add to this that she was ready for the party in a taffeta dress and he was in his chauffeur's uniform, and they made a pretty strange sight. Not quite as strange a sight, though, as Andy and Toby made as they came tumbling and laughing out of the closet.

When the four of them saw each other, they all froze in surprise, and stood there for a long moment with no one saying a word. Andy — always the bold one — broke the ice.

"We were just in the neighborhood and thought we'd drop in," she said.

"B-b-but how did you find the passage?" Charlotte sputtered.

"Oh," Andy said, trying to seem cool, inspecting her nails casually as she spoke, "we just followed your lilac scent."

"Actually," Toby admitted. "We were on the hot trail of a hot iron." She held out her wrinkled outfit by way of explanation. "We more or less tripped onto the secret passageway. It was kind of too much to resist."

Charlotte looked panic-stricken. Clearly she didn't find being discovered at all amusing. She broke away from McNulty quickly and got a furrowed-brow look, as though she were rummaging through her mind for a good lie.

"Steven . . . uh, I mean McNulty here was just showing me how to perform mouth-to-mouth resuscitation, in case any of the older guests pass out at the party. We were just about to move on to the Heimlich maneuver in case anyone chokes at dinner."

"Charlotte," Toby said simply. "You don't have to cook up a lie for our benefit. We won't tell anyone that you two are involved if you don't want us to. We won't even tell Jane."

"Yeah," Andy added, "we're Secrets Specialists. If you don't want us to tell, our lips are sealed as a tomb."

Charlotte looked at them for a good long time, clearly deciding whether or not to trust them.

Finally, she sighed in relief, moved back toward McNulty, wound an arm around his waist, and said, "Jane's okay. You can tell her. I was trying to think of a way to tell her myself. But Mother and Father — well, they have old-fashioned notions about servants, I'm afraid. Even though Steven is an art student, and Mother is devoted to art and artists, it's better if they're from families she knows and enrolled at the Institute, not guys working for her and taking classes at night. The thing is, Steven really needs this job, and I really need Steven. If you told my parents, I'm pretty sure they'd fire him and try to make it hard for us to see each other."

"You've got our word, Charlotte," Toby said, and for the first time since they'd arrived at the Barrett house, she saw Charlotte's usually rigid face open into a really nice smile.

"Call me Char," she said to both of them. "And if there's anything I can do to help you through the party, let me know. I could see at dinner last night that this isn't exactly your usual territory."

"Well, the first thing we need is still an iron," Toby said.

At this request, McNulty stepped forward.

"Let me show them, Char. You'd better get back upstairs before you're missed."

Charlotte was almost out of the room when she hesitated and turned back for a moment.

"Oh, and can you keep the secret passage secret, too? It's how I found Steven in the first place, and now it's how I sneak down to see him. It's been our secret for almost a year now."

"What secret passage?" Andy said, turning to Toby. "I don't recall any secret passage, do you?"

"Secret what?" Toby asked.

CHAPTER ELEVEN

By seven-thirty, Toby and Andy were dressed and on their way downstairs, nervous about the party. By seven-thirty-five, they were standing in the north parlor in their Pilgrim bonnets, feeling ridiculous. The fact that everyone at the party was wearing one of these hats didn't make the girls feel the slightest bit less ridiculous.

Although the party was quite large, it was very sedate. Nothing like the Christmas party at Baker House the term before, which could be heard nearly as far as Greenleaf. Nothing rowdy or obstreperous was going on here. The guests at the Barretts' Landing party were mostly adults, a lot of them older. They were talking to each other in pairs or small groups, sipping wine and eating hors d'oeuvres as the small band played elevator-type music. Toby and Andy tried to get out among them and mingle, so Jane wouldn't think they were punking out.

By eight o'clock, Andy was standing in the corner of the conservatory, holding a cup of punch, being questioned by an elderly woman, another patron of the Smyth Museum.

"Where is it you go to school, my dear?" she asked.

"Canby Hall, ma'am."

"Ah, yes. Isn't that the school young Jane attends? I really should introduce the two of you."

"Thank you, but we're roommates."

"Oh, I see. Well then, you've probably already made each other's acquaintance."

Andy resisted the strong temptation to say, "No. Not yet, actually. It's a large room."

Meanwhile Toby was in the front foyer having a little chat with a tall man who worked at Mr. Barrett's bank. He was interested in the weather in Texas.

"Rather hot down there, I'd think," he said.

"Most of the time," Toby said.

"And sunny?"

"Yes."

"But of course you get rain, too," he said.

"Oh, yes," Toby said.

"But not snow."

"Not where we live," she said, thinking, How much longer can we go on with this?

By eight-fifteen, the two roommates were

having a powwow in the hallway alongside the
front stairs.

"Is this the dullest crowd you've ever seen?"
Toby asked Andy.

"Of *living* people, yes," Andy replied.

Just then Jane came rushing by with the
party photographer in tow.

"I want him to get a shot of the 'tall ship'
cake before we cut it," she said to them in
passing, then as an afterthought asked, "Are
you guys having a good time?"

"Great," Toby lied.

"Terrific," Andy lied even worse.

When they were alone again, Andy looked
around and said, "You know, Tobe, maybe
it's not the crowd. Maybe it's the party. I
mean, how good a time can anyone have while
standing with little sandwiches in their hand
and a Pilgrim hat on their head?"

"Plus they've all known each other a thou-
sand years and probably don't have that much
left to say," Toby added.

Suddenly a voice from behind them was
saying, "And the band is playing those moldy
oldies from the Paleolithic Age. No one could
possibly dance to any of those funeral dirges."

Toby and Andy turned around sharply,
alarmed that they'd been overheard criticizing
the party, and so were relieved to see it was
just Cary. He was taking notes in a little book
— jottings for his anthropology report.

"How do you like my disguise?" he asked

them, slipping the notebook into his jacket pocket. "I came as a Normal Person. Do you think I'll fool anybody?" They had to admit he *did* look extremely normal in a gray suit, white shirt, and maroon tie.

"Don't answer too soon," he warned them. "For beneath Clark Kent's mild-mannered exterior. . . ." He whipped open one side of his jacket to reveal a red and blue suspender with little Superman insignias running down it. Andy and Toby were laughing at this when Mr. Barrett walked up.

"Well, well, so how are things going here in kiddie corner?"

"Fine, Mr. Barrett," the three of them said, almost in unison.

"You youngsters should circulate a little. Talk to some of the grown-ups. You might just get some answers to your questions about corporate law and international banking."

The three of them exchanged furtive looks of disbelief. Then Mrs. Barrett joined them. She asked her husband in a low voice, "David, do you think the party has a certain flatness to it? I mean, do our guests seem to be having fun?"

"Oh, I think so. I myself just had a scintillating conversation with Junior Worthington about his zinnias. He's got a new hybrid this year that sounds spectacular. Of course, maybe a conversation like that wouldn't be *everyone's* idea of fun. Why are you asking, Gloria?"

"Well, for one thing, I just noticed Fred Dunbar napping in the corner of the south parlor. For another, there's a group in the library that's setting up the Parcheesi board. I don't think either of those could be good signs."

"Oooo," Toby whispered to Andy, "but this party just got very fun for me."

"Huh?" Andy said.

"Neal Worthington just walked in the front door."

"So, go get him."

"Too shy," Toby whispered.

In response to this, Andy gave Toby a swift, subtle shove toward the front door, causing her to stumble out to about two feet in front of a surprised Neal.

"Just the person I was most looking forward to finding here," he said, smiling. Which made Toby feel weak in the knees. "Would you care to take a walk through the conservatory with me? I need to warm up and they always save all the heat here for the orchids. You know, sometimes I think the Boston bluebloods got that name from how cold they keep their houses. They're quite a parsimonious bunch, you know."

Toby gave him a question mark look that showed she didn't know what he meant.

"They're a bunch of skinflints," he clarified.

"But they're so rich," Toby said.

"Yes, and how do you think they got that way?" he teased.

"But you're one of them. Does that mean you're a tightwad, too?"

"Well, you may have noticed I've never asked you out on a date to a fancy French restaurant."

"You've never asked me out on *any* date," Toby chided him.

"I haven't? What a terrible oversight. I'll have to correct it immediately. What about next weekend? I could drive up to Canby Hall and take you out to that ultra continental dining spot — Pizza Pete's."

Toby laughed and said, "I accept with pleasure. I won't even bother checking with my social secretary. For you, I'm sure I have room on my calendar."

Toby couldn't believe how easy it was for her to flirt with Neal. The only other boy she'd had any real conversation with was Randy Crowell. Talking with him was easy, too — as long as the subject was horses. When it veered over into the romantic, though, Randy started acting like Toby was his pesky kid sister, and she got all tongue-tied.

Why didn't this happen with Neal? If anything, a guy as rich and sophisticated and cultured as he was ought to make her *more* nervous, especially since he had such formal manners. But the truth about Neal was that just underneath those formal ways was a really warm person. It was probably that warmth that let her talk with him so openly and easily.

By now, they'd wound their way through the crowd and were in the conservatory, a beautiful greenhouse filled with flowers, its glass walls and roof letting in the moonlight.

"This is just so weird and great," Toby said, looking around. "It's like someone set up a piece of summer in the middle of winter."

"You always have such a special way of saying things," Neal told her.

"Me?" Toby said, amazed. "I thought I sounded just like everyone else."

"Oh no. You sound like no one else. Particularly no one else around here. I've spent my whole life with people who sound exactly like each other. And I don't just mean our Boston accents."

"You mean, 'Pahk your cah in Hahvahd Yahd'?" Toby mimicked how he and Jane talked.

"Right. But the way you express yourself is different in more ways than just your Texas drawl. Although I must say that *is* quite attractive."

The only response to this Toby could come up with was a huge blush.

"The curse of being a redhead," she said, smiling bashfully as she realized how red she must be getting.

"The way I see it, that's just another way in

which you're special," Neal said, then rushed in with, "No, no. Forget I said that. I don't want you to be the first person to have to be rushed to Boston General Hospital with acute blushing."

This stopped her blushing and started her laughing. When she stopped, she turned and noticed the most beautiful flowers in the conservatory.

"Oh, look at these!" she exclaimed, pointing to the bed of white orchids.

"Mr. Barrett's pride and joy," Neal said. "He and my father are both heavily into gardening. In fact, I'm surprised my father's not back here already, inspecting things. He must be trying to be social."

"I didn't see him come in with you."

"I dropped him and my mother off, then parked. I'll introduce you. You'd recognize him, anyway, though. We look practically alike, only he's about thirty years older. Sometimes people I've never even met will come up to me and say, 'Aren't you Junior Worthington's son?' "

"Junior?"

"Well, his father was the first Cornelius Worthington, so he got stuck with 'Junior.' I'm Cornelius Worthington III, so I get to just be Neal."

"You're lucky no one started calling you 'Corny,' " she teased.

"Boy, that really would've been awful.

Yeah, they let me take my own nickname. That's about it, though, for independence."

"How do you mean?" Toby asked.

"Well, these old Boston families are very traditional. Sons are expected to follow in their fathers' footsteps. My grandfather started the law firm of Worthington, Barton, and Bellows. My father is the senior partner now. He just assumes I'll go to Harvard like him and then enter the firm. As soon as I've built up my practice a bit, I'll be expected to marry a girl from one of the fifty or so families that 'matter,' as my father would put it. Sometimes he jokingly refers to marriage as 'merging stock portfolios,' but it's not really that much of a joke, if you know what I mean."

"That sounds awful," Toby said. "It's like being handed a script, and all you're supposed to do is read the lines someone else wrote for you."

He looked at her with surprise in his eyes.

"Exactly," he said. "I'd never thought of it quite that way, but that's what it is. You're incredibly perceptive, October."

"Stop," she begged. "You'll just set me off blushing again."

"Come meet my parents," he said. "You'll see better what I mean. Then maybe we could talk about this more next weekend. I really don't feel I have anyone I can explain this to. Everyone around here, at my prep school — well, they don't seem to mind having the way all paved for them. To them, it just makes everything easier, knowing exactly where they're going and how they're going to get there."

"But that doesn't leave any room for surprises," Toby said. "I'm hoping my life will be full of them."

Neal slid into a slow grin, looked down into her eyes, and said, "Toby, you may have a Texas drawl and I may have a Boston accent, but it looks like we definitely speak the same language."

On their way out of the conservatory, they ran into Cary and Jane, who were just coming in.

"Hi, you guys," Jane said, giving Toby a knowing wink.

Toby tried to ignore this, and just said, "Your father's flowers are really beautiful."

"Yeah, that's why we came out here, too," Cary said impishly. "To see the flowers." To underline his point, he put an arm around Jane and gave her a squeeze.

"So you want to see the flowers, eh?" Jane teased Cary when they were in the conservatory.

His reply was to pull her gently by the hand to the other side of the orchids, where he took her arm and draped it over his own shoulder, then leaned toward her and gave her a long kiss.

"I feel like I haven't really seen you the whole weekend, what with the party and all," he said. "You haven't forgotten me in all the commotion, have you?"

Her reply to this was an even longer kiss.

Which, unfortunately, was interrupted in the middle by the sudden appearance — as if out of nowhere — of Mrs. Barrett. By the time they heard her coming, she was already there.

"Jane!" she snapped.

"Oh my," Jane said, jumping back, away from Cary. "Mother."

"Please. Consider appearances. Anyone could walk in here, and what would they find?"

"Me kissing Jane," Cary acknowledged. "And they'd be shocked, I know, because they wouldn't expect such bold behavior from Clark Kent, mild-mannered reporter for the *Daily Planet*. But little do they know that beneath this corporate executive suit and Pilgrim hat beats the heart of that visitor from the planet Krypton — SuperCary!" And with this, he jumped up onto a table and pulled open his suit jacket to reveal his Superman suspenders.

He froze there like that while Jane looked to see what her mother's reaction would be. At first she just stood stock-still and Jane feared she was shocked, or indignant, or both. But then she saw the beginnings of a twinkle creep into her mother's eyes and a smile begin to spread across her face. And then, unable to suppress it any longer, Mrs. Barrett burst out laughing.

"I think, Mr. Slade," she said, "I'm beginning to understand what my daughter sees in you." And then she turned to leave, but only got a few steps before turning back to add, "I assume, of course, that you're going to include this 'participation' of yours into your anthropological report. It's definitely interesting human behavior."

She fixed him with an amused look and held it until he was forced into a sheepish smile. Then he pulled his little notebook out of his pocket, ripped out the scribbled pages, and tore them into tiny pieces, which he dropped into a nearby bin of weeds and clippings.

"Well," he said, taking Jane and her mother by their arms, and guiding them out of the conservatory, "I guess as long as I'm a participant here, I might as well join the party."

CHAPTER
TWELVE

When Cary and Jane came back into the house, Andy, Toby, and Neal were standing in a group, bemoaning what terrible shape the party was in. The doldrums had set in like cement. Quite a few of the guests had already left, and the ones still there were eyeing their watches. Jane's parents were looking around with woebegone expressions on their faces.

Cary scanned the crowd and assessed the situation.

"This party needs intensive care!"

"But what can *we* do?" Andy wondered.

"Yeah," Neal said sarcastically, "I forgot to bring my clown suit."

"And I left my puppet show at school," Toby said.

"Come on, you two," Jane said. "Get serious. We've got to do something drastic — and fast — or this party's going to go down the tubes!"

"I wish the band would stop playing that mush," Cary said, putting his hands over his ears. "It's seeping into my brain cells. It's obstructing my thought processes." He closed his eyes, then he popped them open again and looked back at the band, which was at the moment playing "Tea for Two."

"Hey," he said, an impish grin spreading across his face, "let's see if we can light a little fire under those guys!"

He took off his Pilgrim hat, rushed across the room and up onto the low bandstand, and began having an earnest conversation with the bandleader. Pretty soon, the man was nodding, then smiling, then stopping the band to give new instructions.

Cary rushed back with the news.

"These guys play all sorts of gigs. They've got rock and roll instruments in their van out back — including an extra guitar! They're willing to let me sit in with them. We probably won't sound like the Stones, but we ought to be able to get these people on their feet and get those feet moving."

"I don't know, Cary," Jane said, sounding dubious. "I don't think many of Mother and Father's friends are exactly party maniacs."

"Yeah," Andy added. "I do not see a lot of boogie potential in this group."

"Then you'll have to teach them," Cary said. "You're the disco queen of Canby Hall. You ought to be able to mobilize a few people into a few simple steps."

Andy thought this over, nodded her head, and then ran to the center of the room and shouted, "All right, everybody, it's time for the fun to begin. Step right up for the high point of the evening — Andy's Disco Madness Dance Lessons!"

At first, all her enthusiasm went over like a lead balloon. Of the guests who chose to even notice her, most peered at her with an aloof mixture of amusement and boredom. A lot of people, though, just looked away as if embarrassed, as if Andy were a cheerleader for a team that was losing forty-five to nothing. But Andy was not a girl to give up easily. She ignored this lack of response and jumped from the dance floor up onto the bandstand and grabbed the microphone off its stand.

"I'm not going away," she chided the crowd, "so ignoring me won't work. Now come on. I need a few volunteers. I need some Pilgrims with dancing feet!" She looked down at the crowd and, much to her dismay, saw what looked like an appalled Mrs. Barrett standing against the far wall. Still, Andy had to go on with this. If she stopped now, she would only look foolish. If she could gather up a little momentum and get some of the guests out onto the floor, she might be able to save the party, although not quite in any way Mrs. Barrett would have asked for.

Then Toby and Neal and Jane and Charlotte came to Andy's rescue, moving onto the floor, spreading out, trying to make the dance floor look as full as they could. Amazingly, the other guests who joined them were the older ones.

"What do you think is going on here?" Andy covered the microphone and asked Cary.

"I think the people our parents' age used to be rock and rollers, but now they're older and cooler than all that. You know. But the old folks don't have such a big investment in seeming cool. They can afford to take a chance."

By this time Cary and the band had the instruments in tune and around twenty people were gathered and waiting on the dance floor.

"Can you guys start off with a few slow and easy numbers and then work gradually up to frenzy level?" Andy asked. Cary nodded as she hopped down off the stage, into her small crowd of waiting dance students. As the band started off with a medley of easygoing Motown tunes— "Tracks of My Tears" and "My Girl" and "Where Did Our Love Go?" — Andy got everyone into a line and stood in front of them to show them a few basics.

When she saw how stiff and stilted most of them were, she urged, "The steps aren't all that important. What you mostly want to do is merge your bodies with the music, get behind the sound, close your eyes, and go with the beat." The older guests looked at each other quizzically, but began trying to do what Andy was telling them to. And slowly, things began to happen. The older people put down their Pilgrim hats and bonnets and came into the twentieth century with ear-to-ear smiles. By the time the band had worked its way up to Bruce Springsteen's "Dancing in the Dark," the older dancers had really gotten into the spirit of things, but at the same time they were also beginning to wear down. Gradually they were being replaced on the dance floor by the younger and middle-aged guests, who had apparently decided that by hanging back and being cool and reserved, by standing there like pillars of society, they were missing out on all the fun.

Toby stayed out on the dance floor with Neal, who was so smooth that she almost lost her usual dancing self-consciousness. By following what he did, she felt she was a pretty decent dancer. Jane, meanwhile, was showing her sister and mother some of the newer, trickier moves from Canby Hall and Oakley Prep dances. Mr. Barrett, as usual on his own wavelength, was off by the fireplace, dancing by himself, doing a unique version of the Twist.

By the time the band — with Cary doing

his best Bob Seger imitation — launched into
"Gimme That Old Time Rock and Roll,"
the dancers were packed onto the floor, spill-
ing out into other rooms, into the hallways,
even into the kitchen. Walton the butler had
even set down his tray to dance for a moment
with Bernice the maid. In a far corner of the
dining room, Charlotte was dancing with Mc-
Nulty! Although the solemn spirit of the Barretts' landing in America had gotten lost in
the shuffle, what a shuffle it was. The party
had woken up and come alive and gone totally
wild! So wild, in fact, that one of the unin-
vited neighbors on Louisburg Square called
the Boston police to complain about the noise
level.

Mr. Barrett answered the door, and was
quite surprised to find himself facing the law,
a first in his extremely proper life. He kept a
serious face on and assured the police officer
that he would quiet things down a bit. But
when the door had closed behind the cops,
he gave them a mock salute, and said, "See you
later, alligators."

He turned with a boyish grin to tell Jane
and Charlotte and Mrs. Barrett, "I guess
we're just too wild for the neighborhood."

"Right you are, Mr. Barrett," said Andy,
who had come out into the hall with Toby
and Neal to see what was happening. "This
party is simply too *bodacious*."

"You took the words right out of my mouth, Andrea," Mr. Barrett said, which caused all of them to crack up.

Later, much later, into the wee hours of the morning after the band had pleaded exhaustion and the last of the guests — Cary and Neal among them — had gone home, the Barretts and Andy and Toby gathered in the kitchen. Mrs. Barrett sent the servants on to bed.

"We'll forage around and find a snack ourselves," she told Walton and Bernice.

"If anyone's interested," Toby ventured. "I can fix my specialty — huevos rancheros."

"Huevos what?" Jane said.

"It's sort of Mexican breakfast. Fried eggs with a tomato-and-onion hot sauce. You wouldn't happen to have any tortillas in here, would you?" she asked, poking around in the huge refrigerator.

"I'm not sure you could find a tortilla on all of Beacon Hill," Jane said. "To folks around here, a hamburger is pretty much as ethnic as their eating gets."

"Then we can make do with toast. What about refried beans? Do you think there's a can or two around here?"

"There might be some Boston baked beans in the pantry," Mrs. Barrett said.

"Well," Toby sighed, "it'll be a pretty weird

Mexican breakfast, but if anybody's interested, I'll give it a try."

"Yeah, Toby!" Jane said and everyone else joined in, helping by finding the ingredients, chopping onions and tomatoes, and keeping hot slices of bread popping out of the toaster. Within twenty minutes, they were all sitting around the big kitchen table, Mr. Barrett in his shirt and suspenders, his tie unknotted, Mrs. Barrett and the girls with their shoes kicked off, enjoying an informal and — everyone laughingly agreed — pretty weird breakfast.

"I've got to hand it to you girls," Mr. Barrett said to Toby and Andy and Jane, "you and Cary really put the party back on its feet."

"Oh, but are those feet aching now," Charlotte said, adding a joking moan.

"Well, I'm not surprised you've got sore peds," Jane teased her. "You were a dancing maniac out there tonight. I think you danced with everyone at the party. Didn't I even see you dancing with McNulty at one point?"

Toby and Andy simultaneously gulped mouthfuls of coffee. They hadn't had a chance yet, in all the commotion, to tip Jane off about Charlotte and her boyfriend. And Charlotte was clearly thrown off by Jane's innocent observation.

But then, unexpectedly, Mrs. Barrett

chimed in with, "I danced one number with him myself. Did you know he's an artist? Quite talented, too, I gather. He's been in a couple of group shows here. Tonight's the first time I think I've ever really talked to him about himself. A very interesting young man, I must say."

Toby and Andy smiled conspiratorially across the table at Charlotte, who said, "Yes. He seemed rather interesting to me, too."

"Hmm," Mrs. Barrett said, distracted by her huevos rancheros. "So this is how you eat, Texas-style?"

Toby and Andy grinned in response to the tease. It had to mean that Mrs. Barrett had come to like them.

"Well, I did make a few substitutions, ma'am," Toby said. "But, yep, this is your basic Tex-Mex breakfast."

"Well, it's quite good," Mrs. Barrett said. "Around here, we usually have poached eggs for Sunday breakfast. Of course, we usually have Sunday breakfast at ten A.M., not four A.M. You girls are shaking us out of our settled ways."

"Not to mention adding new challenges to my chess game," Mr. Barrett added. Which struck terror in Toby and Andy's hearts until they looked up and saw that he was grinning slyly as he said this.

As the girls finished their coffee and excused themselves to go upstairs, Mr. and Mrs.

Barrett were still going strong with a hilarious recap of the party.

"Did you see Rose Henderson doing the frug, or whatever it was — something very sixties and psychedelic — with old Horace Busby?" Mrs. Barrett asked, and went into peals of laughter at the memory.

"Mother and Father had such a great time," Jane said to Andy and Toby as the three of them slowly climbed the stairs. "And it was all thanks to you." She put an arm around each of them and gave them a hug. As a Barrett, I thank you for making the Landing party a success."

"Just thank us as yourself," Andy said. "That's what we love you for. For being a terrific *you*. Not because you belong to an important family."

"But being a Barrett is one of the most important things about me," Jane said.

"No," Andy contested her. "Being a Barrett is an *interesting* thing about you. An important thing about you is that you're a talented writer. That you have a great sense of humor."

"That you're a flash card maniac," Toby said.

"And a total slob in the room," Andy added to the teasing.

Jane gave them both fake punches in the arm as they reached the second-floor landing.

Before she went through the door to her room, she turned and told them, "You know, I think you two are more important to me than I even knew."

And then, just as she was about to shut her door behind her, Toby whispered across the carpeted hallway, "Remind us to tell you Charlotte's secret."

Instantly, Jane popped back out into the hall.

"*What* secret?"

Toby faked a large yawn, stretched her arms over her head, and said, "Too tired now. You'll have to wait until tomorrow."

"You guys!" Jane called out to them, but they were already up the stairs and out of sight.

CHAPTER THIRTEEN

After sincerely fond farewells with Mr. and Mrs. Barrett, and a few secret-keeping looks with Charlotte, Toby and Andy climbed into the backseat of Cary's red Toyota, where he and Jane were already waiting, in the front seat, whispering and holding hands and laughing at their own private jokes.

"All right, all right," Andy said as she crawled into the back, "stop with the mushy stuff. The backseat drivers have arrived." Jane turned to look at the large paper bundle Toby was dragging in behind her.

"What's that?" Jane asked.

"You'll see," Toby said mysteriously, patting the bag, which took up nearly a third of the backseat and held the rainbow bedspread and rug she had bought the day before.

"Hmmm," Jane said. "Seems like there are a *couple* of secrets I'm going to have to wring out of you two." And she grabbed the first possible opportunity to do just that.

As soon as they'd reached Canby Hall and Cary had let them out in front of Baker, she turned to them and asked, "Okay, so what's the story on Charlotte?"

"McNulty," Andy said as cryptically as she could. For her, a big part of gossip — or "dishing," as she called it — was dangling her information tantalizingly in front of the person interested in it.

"What *about* McNulty? What connection could there possibly be between him and Charlotte?" Jane asked, rising to the bait. In response, Andy just started whistling and looking aimlessly around the campus.

"*No!*" Jane gasped, floored by the information.

"Oh yes," Andy said. "True love."

"How do you know?"

Toby jumped in and told Jane the whole story.

"Secret passage? McNulty?!" Jane exclaimed. "This is too much."

"She told us to tell you, Jane," Andy added. "But *not* your parents. Although it looks like your mother warmed up to him a little at the party. At least she began to see him as a real person, and not just the guy behind the wheel."

"McNulty," Jane said again, still trying to wrap her mind around this piece of information. "Well, he is kind of cute, in his own way, isn't he?"

"If you mean the Scrawny-Guy-with-Thick-Glasses kind of way, he's positively gorgeous," Andy said.

"Come on. He's all right," Jane said, talking herself into McNulty's merits. "And he's about as tall as Charlotte, don't you think?"

"Oh yeah," said Toby this time, "if she's sitting down and he's standing on a box."

"You two!" Jane said. "You can't honestly care about such superficial things?"

"No, we honestly don't," Andy said. "And more important, the two of them don't, either. They've got to know they make a pretty funny-looking couple, but as far as I can tell, they're the ones who are laughing the hardest — between kisses, of course!"

"McNulty and Charlotte," Jane muttered, still working it through her mind. Suddenly she turned and punched the huge paper bag Toby was lugging up the steps. "Now I've got to see what's in here!" she said, as she grabbed it and ran inside with it. Toby ran after her and Andy ran in after Toby. As soon as their feet hit the highly waxed floor of the Baker House lobby, the three of them went into a giant skid, which landed them in a heap of uncontrollable laughter on top of the bundle. They were just coming down off this giggle high when they heard a cold voice from above them ticking off their names.

"Andrea Cord. October Houston. Jane Barrett."

They looked up. It was Meredith Pembroke, a person they had nearly managed to forget in the past two days.

"Yes, Ms. Pembroke?" Jane said, as politely as she could.

"I'm afraid all three of you signed the weekend sign-out sheet in pencil. Signing out requires ink, as you would know if you read your Canby Hall rule book. I'm going to have to give each of you a demerit."

All three of them groaned in unison.

"Please don't do that," Meredith said. "I don't want to have to penalize you another two demerits for insubordination." And with that, she walked away, marking down their infractions and demerits on her clipboard as she went.

"Great to be back," Andy said sarcastically when Meredith was gone.

"Yeah," Jane added. "Welcome Wagon ought to hire her. She's got a way of making a person feel right at home."

"Come on, you guys," Toby urged. "Let's haul our stuff up to the old bunkhouse. If we sit here ten seconds longer, she's liable to come back and give us a few demerits for loitering."

On their way back to their room, the roommates passed the open door of 409. Inside the room, Dee and Maggie were studying, but looked up when they heard their friends in the hall.

"Home are the weary partiers," Dee said.

"Yeah," Maggie said. "You guys look like it was hard duty."

"Oh no," Toby said, coming in and flopping onto Dee's bed. "The party was great. It's the management around this place."

"We just had a run-in with our lovely new housemother," Jane explained.

"Join the club," Maggie said. "We're thinking of papering our walls with all the demerits we've collected. Everything's a crime around here now. You can't even breathe around Baker anymore. I think she's found some ancient rule that forbids breathing."

"What's her problem?" Andy wondered, dragging in the bag with Toby's bedspread in it and sitting on it as though it were a portable chair.

"There are a few rumors going around. One's that she really *was* a prison warden before she came here. Another has it that she drinks lemon juice for breakfast every morning to give herself a sour disposition. And then somebody said her older cousin's roommate went to school with someone named Meredith Pembroke someplace in New Hampshire, and she was the wildest girl in the history of the school."

"Must've been another Meredith Pembroke," Jane said.

"That's what we figured," Dee said, speaking for her and Maggie.

"What's everybody doing about this?" Andy asked.

"Lying low," Maggie said. 'You can hear a pin drop in the halls. Everyone's just staying in their rooms, or out of Baker until curfew."

"Well, that's what we'll do, too," Toby said. "We'll beat Ms. Pembroke at her own game. We'll be so good that she won't be able to find a rule we're breaking."

Toby's plan went perfectly, for about twelve hours. During that time, she studied, then slept, then got up for classes. She wasn't out of her room ten minutes before she had her next demerit from Meredith.

"What's this for?" she said, looking incredulously at the pink slip she'd just been handed by the housemother, as she stood drying her hair in front of the mirrors in the fourth floor bathroom.

"No electric appliances allowed in the dorm," Meredith said tersely.

"That means hotplates and refrigerators, not a little blow dryer," Toby protested. "Everyone in the dorm uses them. Except the girls who use hot rollers and curling irons."

"Then they'll all get demerits," Meredith said simply. "As soon as I catch them." And then she just walked out.

* * *

As the week passed, things went from bad to worse and then to worse yet.

On Monday night, Andy risked a late night call to keep her promise to Faith and tell her all about the weekend in Boston. She was just hanging up when, from behind her back, she heard the sickeningly familiar sound of Meredith Pembroke ripping another pink demerit slip off the top of her pad.

On Tuesday morning, Meredith sprung a surprise room check on the fourth floor. She found Jane's part of 407 in its usual state — National Disaster Area — with unmade bed and shoes in piles on the closet floor and twenty-seven empty soda cans abandoned in various spots.

"I clean up on Saturday mornings," Jane told Meredith, trying to get her to soften up a little.

"Too bad," Meredith said with false sympathy. "If only I'd picked the right day, the room would doubtless have passed with flying colors. As it is, though, I'm going to give each of you three demerits."

"But that's not fair!" Jane shouted. "The mess is all mine."

"All roommates are responsible for the condition and appearance of the room," Meredith said, and then when none of the roommates could break out of their speechless anger, she added. "I just go by the rule book."

She looked around the room before leaving and said, "I love the rainbows, though."

On Wednesday night, Jane was given five more demerits when Meredith found her and Cary kissing good-night on the front steps of the dorm.

"Public displays of affection are expressly forbidden in Section 7 of the rule book," she informed them.

"Surely she's joking," Cary said when Meredith had gone off.

"I'm afraid not," Jane said glumly. "Or else she has the weirdest sense of humor on Earth. Actually, we keep *hoping* she's from another planet and will find her spacecraft and leave soon, but instead she seems to be sticking around."

On Thursday afternoon, Andy came back from classes to find three fresh demerits waiting on her desk for "unauthorized keeping of pet in room."

"She means Hector!" Andy wailed, rushing over to the bowl where Hector, a goldfish she'd gotten at the Woolworth's in Greenleaf, was happily swimming around, completely unaware that he was unauthorized.

"This is the last straw!" she said to Toby and Jane, slamming her fist on the window-sill next to Hector's bowl.

"Oh, don't worry," Jane tried to console

her. "I've got more demerits than you and they haven't locked me up yet."

"Yeah," Andy said. "I've been meaning to ask you that — just exactly how do these demerits add up? Alison never gave them, so I really don't know. I hope it's not that if you get fifteen, you have to go to federal prison, because I've got fourteen at the moment."

"If you get twenty you have to go before the all-campus board. That's all the houseparents and Ms. Allardyce, of course," Jane said. Patrice Allardyce was the headmistress of Canby Hall. A cool, icy blonde with a regal bearing, she was strict, but usually fair with the girls.

"P.A.!" Andy shouted, using the nickname by which Ms. Allardyce was referred to — behind her back, that is. "Maybe she's our answer."

"How?" Toby said, left behind by Andy's train of thought. "You're going to go and have a cozy little chat with her, over a cup of tea? Tell her our troubles with our housemother? P.A. goes by the same rule book that Meredith does."

"But she applies them fair and square," Jane said. "I think Andy might be right. I think that if P.A. knew about Meredith's demerit rampage, she might see our side. She doesn't want every girl at Canby Hall to get expelled. Which is what's eventually going to happen if Meredith keeps passing out pink slips like she has been. The school will be empty. Canby Hall will have to shut down."

"I don't think it'll get quite that far," Andy said, seeing that Jane had gotten on a roll. "But it might be worth a trip across campus to plead our case. Of course, Jane, you're so articulate, I really think it should be *you* who goes to see P.A."

"Oh no, it was your idea, Ms. Cord. And besides, I think it'll look better if the three of us go together. That way it won't look like just one of us has sour grapes."

Toby nodded and said all right, she'd go.

"Okay," Andy said. "Me, too. But let's do it now, while our nerve is up. If you give me a day to think over a visit to Patrice Allardyce, I'll probably back out."

Patrice Allardyce lived in the headmistress's residence on the edge of campus, over by the skating pond. It was a beautiful Victorian frame house painted white with wine-colored shutters and trim. A wide porch circled from the front around the side. As the three roommates approached it now in the late winter afternoon, small wisps of smoke were coming out of the chimney, which meant that Ms. Allardyce had a fire going in her study. The lights from that room and the parlor glowed warmly out onto the gray campus.

Toby, Andy, and Jane stood hesitantly on the porch in front of Patrice Allardyce's door.

"Well, come on," said Toby, whose teeth were chattering even though she had suited up in jeans and a down jacket and leg warmers and moon boots. "If we don't get out of this cold soon, this Texan is going to freeze to death."

Jane nodded and pushed the doorbell. From within, footsteps grew closer and closer, and then Patrice Allardyce was opening the door to them. She was dressed more casually than they were used to seeing her. She looked a lot less severe than usual in plain navy pants and a comfortably stretched-out old turtleneck that was streaked with what looked like flour and spice dust. Exotic spice smells were emanating from within. Andy the detective deduced that Ms. Allardyce was in the midst of some fancy cooking — but what kind? She put her nose up into the air and sniffed. Coming from a restaurant family, Andy prided herself on being able to tell any ethnic cuisine from forty paces.

"Indian," she said now, confidently.

Patrice Allardyce smiled and said, "Yes. A friend gave me an Indian cookbook. I'm working my way through it recipe by recipe. Tonight, if all goes well, tandoori chicken will be emerging from my oven in — " she stopped to check her watch — "twenty-seven minutes. Now. What can I do for you girls?"

"Uh, well . . ." said Jane, who suddenly felt as though the usual bunch of words in her head had fallen through a trap door.

"We need to talk to you," Toby filled in.

"We've got a problem," Andy added.

Ms. Allardyce looked at them and, seeing from the seriousness of their expressions that this was something important, stepped back and said, "Come in, then. Let's go into my study."

When the girls had taken off their jackets and sat down nervously, side by side on the navy velvet sofa facing Ms. Allardyce's desk, Toby once again found herself taking the lead.

"It's about our new housemother," she said. "I'm not sure how to say this so it doesn't sound like namby-pamby whining, but the fact is she's giving out so many demerits that — by my figuring — every girl in Baker will be expelled by March."

At this point, Andy leaped in with some examples, and Jane added a few of her own.

Patrice Allardyce sat silent through their whole protest, her elbows on her desk, her hands under her chin, the fingertips of one pressed against those of the other. Her "deep-thinking" position. Finally she spoke.

"This isn't the first I've heard about this matter. Other girls have come here before you. Technically, though, you do realize that Meredith is in the right. She's going strictly by the Canby Hall rule book."

"*Strictly* is right," Andy said bitterly.

Ms. Allardyce put up a silencing hand.

"Yes, Andrea, you're right. At any rate, she's applying a stricter interpretation of the rules than Alison did. But then Meredith hasn't been here very long. Sometimes in new situations, people don't want to fall short of the mark, and so they wind up shooting way past it. I'm sure you've done the same thing yourselves. Think back to your first weeks here at Canby Hall."

"Yes," Jane admitted. "I overstudied. Maybe I let my highlighting run away with me. But that was just being rough on *myself* — not on a whole dorm-full of girls! Meredith Pembroke is a menace to the great spirit of Baker House. Until she got here, it was the best dorm on campus. Now the girls from Addison and Charles Houses tease us all the time. You know. How are things on Alcatraz?"

"Yes," Andy pleaded. "Please do something about this."

Patrice Allardyce nodded, but said only, "We'll see."

The three roommates fell silent. "We'll see" was not exactly what they'd been hoping for.

"I can tell you're disappointed," Ms. Allardyce said, standing up behind her desk to show the conversation was coming to an end. "But you'll just have to trust me. Sometimes when the dust settles, things have a way of resolving themselves. Which would be much better than me coming in with a heavy hand and resolving them myself. I don't think the dust has settled around Meredith Pembroke. And I think it may be quite interesting to see what's there when it does."

CHAPTER FOURTEEN

Saturday morning Toby woke up to the sound of paper crinkling underneath her cheek. She lifted her head and peered blearily down at the square dusty blue envelope. At first she couldn't imagine what it was, or what it was doing on her pillow. Then it all came back to her slowly. It was Neal's letter. A smile washed over her sleepy face, remembering how she'd found it the day before.

She hardly ever checked her mail slot on the way in from classes. She almost never got any mail, and hated looking, only to find the cubbyhole marked "Houston" empty, surrounded by others stuffed full of funny cards from friends and letters full of photos from parents. She knew her dad loved her a lot, but unfortunately, he was about as expressive as she was. Once every two weeks she got a terse, three or four paragraph letter from him about what was happening at the ranch. In return, she sent him two or three paragraphs about her classes. She had just heard from him earlier in the week and so she wasn't even going to bother checking for mail. She only stopped in the mailroom to look at the bulletin board and see what movie the Film Society had scheduled for the weekend.

And so she was surprised to find the blue envelope there. At first she thought it must be for one of the other girls and had been put in her slot by mistake. That happened sometimes. But no, it was addressed to her, in black ink. A thick, bold script. No return address. A Boston postmark. She slid her finger under the flap and ripped it open. Inside was a single sheet of heavy paper in a matching blue. She unfolded it. The message was only two lines long.

It read: "I seem to be spending most of my time this week missing you. Saturday can't come soon enough. See you then."

It was signed "Neal."

She went to sleep Friday night on the waves of this note, and woke on Saturday feeling even wilder and crazier. Not the kind of crazy where someone was going to have to put her in a straitjacket. More the kind of crazy where she simply had to get outside, into the day, and breathe the fresh winter air, preferably on horseback, riding along, shouting "Yeeeeeee!!!" at the top of her lungs, until she burnt off some of this excess of feeling.

She got up and went to the window and looked out over the campus. It was still gray; the pale winter sun was still behind one of the low rolling Massachusetts hills in the distance. She went to her closet, and quietly, so as not to wake Jane or Andy, put on thermal underwear and old jeans and her heaviest flannel shirt. She pulled on her winter boots, found her down vest under her bed, and slipped out of the room.

First she went down to the Ping-Pong room and got a cup of black coffee and a rocklike doughnut from the machines, gulping them as she headed back up to the lobby and out the front door. As she came down the front steps, she noticed a car pulling in through the Canby Hall gates and up the drive to Baker House. As it got closer, she saw that it was Meredith Pembroke's old Camaro.

When the car pulled up in front of the dorm, Toby could see that there were two people inside. Meredith got out of the driver's seat, laughing at something, and then another woman emerged from the passenger side, laughing even harder. She was about Meredith's age, but not at all like her in style. This woman was very hip in parachute pants and a forties tweed overcoat and bright red rubber boots, the zip-up kind like kindergarteners wear. Her hair was cut in a punky crewcut with a little tail braid at the back of her neck.

She wore glasses with clear red frames. Toby couldn't imagine what a woman like this could possibly have in common with Meredith, and yet here they were, laughing like they were the best of friends. The pieces of the puzzle did not fit.

Meredith's laughter stopped abruptly when she saw Toby. She momentarily left her friend and came around the car, up onto the steps in front of Toby.

"And where, may I ask, do you think you're going at this hour?"

"Riding," Toby answered simply. She had nothing to hide. "I have a friend who lives out on the County Road. His family has a horse farm, and I ride there quite a bit."

"This early?"

"Sometimes I get up and need to be outside. Part of growing up on a ranch, I guess. I can't stand being cooped up all the time. I need blue skies above me."

Meredith looked upward, and said. "The problem, October, is that these skies are not yet blue. Canby Hall rules strictly forbid girls leaving their dorms this early, even if they're just staying on campus, which you have revealed to me was not your intention. This means I'm going to have to give you two demerits instead of one."

Toby glared at Meredith with fire in her eyes, but was met with a stony stare. Clearly, Meredith was not going to back down. Well, so what? Toby thought. I've already got a stack of deremits. What's two more?

"If you'll excuse me, then, ma'am," Toby said, walking around Meredith, and down the steps.

Meredith turned and shouted out to her, "Stop right there, Ms. Houston!"

Toby turned.

"I thought I just told you that you were in violation of school rules."

"Yes," Toby said. "And I just figured as long as I'd already broken them and taken the demerits, I might as well at least get my ride out of it."

"I won't stand for this kind of insubordination," Meredith said. "Get back up those steps. And don't let me see you outside until classes on Monday. You are campused for the rest of the weekend!"

Toby looked at Meredith at first with disbelief in her eyes, then with tears.

"This isn't fair, and you know it!" she shouted at Meredith before she turned and tromped back up the steps and into the dorm. As she went she could hear Meredith's friend speak from behind her.

"Merry! What's the deal here? You trying out for the part of Wicked Witch of the West?"

"She was breaking the rules," Meredith told her friend in a firm voice.

"Yeah, well, if you'll stretch your memory

back a few years, you might remember someone who made a personal campaign to break
every rule in our school rule book — and did.
Plus breaking two rules the administration
had to *invent* to cover stunts of yours they
hadn't had the imagination to think of in
advance!"

"Rachel! Shhh!" Meredith said, but it was
too late. Toby had already heard. What did
this mean, though? Surely this woman had to
be kidding. There was no way Meredith Pembroke could have ever broken so much as one
tiny rule in her entire life.

Toby, however, was about to break two or
three more. She was walking in the front door
of Baker and then sneaking right out the back.

She ran like a shot into the woods bordering
Canby Hall, then up over the two hills to the
Crowell farm. By the time she got there, she
was winded and flushed, and cooled out a little on Meredith.

As she approached the farmhouse, she was
happy to see smoke coming from the kitchen
chimney. That meant Mrs. Crowell was already fixing breakfast for the family. She went
around to the kitchen door and knocked.
Mr. Crowell, Randy's dad, answered. Toby
asked if Randy was up yet.

"I should hope so," Mr. Crowell said. "We
started chores two hours ago here. We're just
stopping for breakfast."

"Is that Toby?" came Mrs. Crowell's voice

from within. "Tell her to come in and have some flapjacks with us. Put some meat on her bones."

"No thanks, Mrs. Crowell," Toby shouted. "I already had breakfast. I just came by to see if Randy would let me give Maxine a workout. I thought maybe she was getting fat on all this winter hay and barn loafing."

"Randy's upstairs, Toby," Mr. Crowell said. "Go on over and saddle Maxine up. I'll tell him you're here."

A few minutes later, as Toby got Maxine ready, Randy came into the barn.

"Are you sure you can handle her in all this snow?" he said, worry in his voice. "I know you're the greatest horsewoman since Annie Oakley, but the hard ground of Texas is a mite different from this. You can't tell where the snow gets deep, or where there are patches of ice underneath it."

"Oh Randy, come on," Toby groaned, rolling her eyes. "You're always big brothering me."

"That's what I'm here for, October," he teased. "To provide you with the wisdom of my years and experience."

"Yeah," she said sarcastically, giving him a fake kick in the shins to emphasize her point, "by bullying me and babying me and generally giving me a hard time. You know darn well I can handle any horse on any terrain in any weather. But here you are, treating me like I'm a nine-year-old and you don't know if you should let me go on the merry-go-round."

"Oh, all right," Randy said. "You win. But please use a little more caution out there today than you usually do."

"Oh no. Today I'll probably exercise no caution at all. Today I am probably going to be totally foolish and crazy."

"Why?" said Randy, mystified.

"I think I'm in love," Toby said, testing out the words as she said them.

"With who?" he asked.

"With *whom*. We learned that in English last week. When it's a direct object — "

"Yeah, yeah, stop ducking my question. Who's this poor guy you've decided you're in love with?"

"Neal Worthington. The most exceptionally cool guy in Boston."

"Oh. How long have you been seeing Mr. Cool?"

"Well, not all *that* long. We're actually only having our first real date tonight. That is, if I can sneak out of Baker again. Meredith Pembroke is really on my case and — "

"Wait a minute." Randy stopped her by gently pressing his hand over her mouth. "October. How can you be in love with someone you haven't even been out with yet? Love is something that has to grow between a guy and a girl as they get to really know each other over a period of time. I think maybe what you mean is that you're *attracted* to this guy."

Toby pulled his hand off her mouth and snapped at him.

"Words, words, words! You're just trying to trip me up on them. But you can't trip me up on my feelings. I know what I feel. You think you're so much older and wiser. Well, I'm telling you I can do just fine without all your advice. I'd prefer to figure out life for myself if you don't mind, even if I have to make all the mistakes you could so nicely save me from."

She could feel her ears burning as she pulled the cinch tight under Maxine's saddle, swung up into it, and rode out of the barn before Randy could come up with a reply.

As she headed out through the corral, she could hear him sputtering after her, "But October, all I meant was. . . ."

Why was everyone on her about everything these days? Don't leave the dorm. You don't know what love is. Be careful not to fall off your horse. Blah. Blah. Blah.

"Come on, Maxine — heeeaaaah!!" she shouted, pressing her knees into the horse's flanks, getting her up to a hard gallop, leaving all the criticism and well-intentioned advice behind her.

She completely ignored Randy's warnings. What she needed right now was a full-tilt, pull-out-all-the-stops ride. The sun was coming up now, making the snow-covered hills and valleys glisten, as though diamond dust had been scattered over them. She rode Maxine hard up the hills, and gave her a free rein barreling down them. The icy wind took the fire out of her, and the freedom of being on horseback made her begin to feel like her regular self again.

Just as she was deciding to slow down a little and think about coming back in, Maxine took off across what looked like a smooth plain at the foot of a hill. In an instant, everything went wrong. Suddenly there was no ground beneath the horse's hooves. They'd run into a bottomless drift. Maxine panicked and flipped over head-first into the snow. Toby wasn't so lucky. In flying off the horse, she was thrown past a tree. Her left foot hit the trunk, and when she tried to get up, an excruciating pain shot through her ankle. She lay back down.

There was nothing but snow beneath her. Suddenly she was very scared. She knew dust storms and rattlesnakes and floods, and had once even come a little too close to a mountain lion. But snow was one fact of nature she knew nothing about. What if she sank down into it, like quicksand?

She tried not to panic. She tried to stay as still as she could. Maybe if she could pull herself upright by the tree, she could walk lightly on the crusty surface of the snow. She made a move to stand and winced in pain again. Something was definitely wrong with her ankle.

Maybe she could crawl to solid ground. But when she tried to roll over onto her stomach, the sharp pain cut short that plan, too. She looked around for Maxine, but the horse had run off somewhere. As brave and fiercely independent as Toby was, she was also smart enough to know when she was in over her head. If she couldn't save herself, she'd have to try to get someone else to come to her rescue. Slowly she raised herself up onto her elbows and took a deep breath.

"Help!" she shouted plaintively to the windy, snowy, deserted countryside. "Help!"

CHAPTER FIFTEEN

After a while, Toby's shouting for help started to wear her out, and began to seem pointless as well. Time started to blur for her. She tried to keep her mind focused, but this became more and more difficult. A couple of times she gingerly tried moving her ankle. She figured that if she could still feel pain, at least she didn't have frostbite.

Gradually, though, all her worrying about frostbite and no one finding her began to ebb away, replaced by a sensation of deep peace and sleepiness.

Maybe I'll just curl up here and take a little nap, she thought, ignoring the small distant voice way in the back of her mind that was saying this probably wasn't such a great idea. She put her head down onto the snow and closed her eyes. Sleep was overtaking her. It was all she could think of.

Then, suddenly, a shouting started up, distant, but definitely not just in her mind.

"October! Toby! Where are you?"

She smiled. Randy. Her big brother, coming to rescue her. She closed her eyes again, thinking, isn't that nice of him. I'll talk to him after my little nap.

And then it hit her like a bolt of lightning. She wasn't just sleepy. She was sinking into unconsciousness. And if she did, Randy might not see her. And then she remembered that her down vest was white, her jeans black. To a distant passing horseman, she might just look like a clump of snow and a couple of fallen branches. Somehow she had to manage to call up enough strength to prop herself up and shout again.

But she couldn't. Her arms felt like Jell-O. The best she could do was roll over on her side. She began shouting.

"Randy. Over here." But even in her foggy mind, she knew that what was coming out was barely above a whisper. She was going to have to do better than this. She took a deep breath and tried again.

"Randy! Over here!" This time she knew she was actually shouting, if weakly. She looked up and saw him. He was still maybe two hundred feet away. She thought for a moment, then smiled, remembering the red wool scarf she had wound around her neck before leaving Baker and stuffed inside the down vest.

Now she reached in and pulled it out and, with the last burst of energy she had in her, waved it aloft as she cried out, "Randy!"

He turned and saw her and reined his horse over in her direction. When he got to her, he jumped off the horse and dropped to his knees beside her.

"October! Are you okay?"

All she could do was shake her head no, and begin to cry with relief that he'd found her. He picked her up gently and carried her over to his horse.

"Do you think anything's broken?" he asked.

"Something's wrong with my ankle," she said.

"Let's get you back," he said. "The ankle looks bad, and I'm also worried you might be suffering from exposure."

He draped her over the saddle, then pulled himself up onto the horse behind her and propped her against himself. He turned the horse in the opposite direction from his family farm.

"I'd better take you back to Canby Hall. The infirmary there is about the closest place we can get you some medical attention."

He rode them in as fast as he could, while at the same time trying to keep Toby from getting jostled. They reached the campus in fifteen minutes or so. About half the time Toby was aware of the ride; the rest of the time she felt spaced out, like the scenery was passing in a blur.

Meanwhile, Meredith Pembroke was taking her friend Rachel across campus to the dining hall for breakfast. The two friends were talking and laughing about old times when suddenly there was a galloping horse thundering through the gates onto the campus.

"*Now* what?!" Meredith said, exasperated. She raised her hand to stop the horse and its riders. Randy reined up in front of her.

"It looks like I'm going to have to give someone a demerit for having livestock on campus," she said. Then, seeing that it was Toby on the horse, she grew incensed.

"Just what's going on here? I thought I campused you this morning, Ms. Houston. I'm afraid I'm going to have to deal out more serious punishment than just demerits to make an impression on you."

Toby just nodded groggily. Meredith saw now that something was wrong.

"What's the matter? Has she been hurt?" Meredith asked Randy. He nodded.

"She's been thrown from a horse, and has been lying in a snowbank a little too long."

"You'd better get her to the infirmary," Meredith said.

"I was just on my way," Randy told her.

"I'll deal with her infraction later. She'll still have to take responsibility for her disobedience."

"Yeah," Randy said angrily. "Well, at least Toby saved you the trouble of campusing her. I think her ankle's going to ground her for a while without any help from you." He nudged his horse into a trot, and rode off.

CHAPTER SIXTEEN

The Canby Hall infirmary was located in one of the school's original buildings, dating from the turn of the century. Inside, it smelled of rubbing alcohol and camphor and bleached bandages — the scents of years and years of broken arms set, fevers quenched, bee stings soothed, generations of girls patched up and sent back off to classes.

On the first floor was a small waiting room, which was quickly becoming full of Toby's friends. Andy and Jane had come as soon as they got the call from Randy. Dee and Maggie had joined them a little while later. They were all waiting, mostly in silence, for word on Toby, who was in one of the upstairs rooms.

By now, the waiting room had a tense air. They had all been sitting in suspense for what seemed like the forever it took Dr. Harvey to drive in from Greenleaf. Now they were wait-

ing through another forever while he was upstairs with Toby.

Finally, he came down the stairs with heavy,
thudding steps, his doctor bag in hand, his
stethoscope still dangling from his neck under
his open overcoat.

"Well, she's going to be just fine," he an-
nounced in a hearty, booming voice. "Right
as rain. Of course she's going to have to rest
up for the next few days, and stay off that
ankle. She's taken a bad sprain. I put a soft
cast on her. Make sure she keeps it dry, Nurse,
and have her use a cane to get around for a
while."

"Yes, Doctor."

"And she probably shouldn't go horseback
riding again this afternoon," he added, with
a broad wink at everyone gathered in the
waiting room.

"Uh, can I go up and see her for a minute?"
Randy asked shyly.

"You the fella who rescued her?" Dr.
Harvey asked.

"Yes."

"Well, I guess knights in shining armor are
due special privileges. But just for a minute. I
gave her a sedative so she'll probably sleep
through until dinnertime."

Randy nodded and leaped to his feet, then
took the steps up two at a time. He pushed
open the door to Toby's room. It looked like
she was almost asleep already.

"Naptime?" he said, pulling up a chair next to her bed.

She nodded. "Sleepy," she said. "Hey. How'd you know to come out after me? How'd you know I was in trouble?"

"Maxine came back to the barn, conspicuously missing a rider. I hightailed it out there as fast as I could."

"Hightailed it," she said groggily, smiling. "A Texas expression. You got that from me, I'll bet."

"Probably. I get a lot from you. I'm not just a smug big brother. You've taught me as much, maybe more, than I've taught you. And as for my advice to the lovelorn — forget it. I think I just got so burned by Dana, my old Canby Hall flame, falling for her so fast and then going through such a long broken heart afterward, that I was trying to protect you from a similar mistake. But you're right. You've got to have your own experiences."

Toby smiled sleepily and teased, "Including getting myself thrown from a few horses."

"We'll get you on the horse that threw you as soon as you're better. By the way, Maxine says she's sorry."

Meanwhile, downstairs in the waiting room, a new visitor had shown up. Meredith Pembroke. Toby's friends fell into silence as she came through the door with her friend. Nurse Zinger met them in the foyer.

"I'd like to see October Houston," Meredith said commandingly.

"Sorry. No more visitors this afternoon. Doctor's orders," Nurse Zinger told Meredith in her official nurse tone of voice, which she was especially good at. "But it's just as well you came by. I need your signature on the accident report. And I'd like you to call the girl's father, let him know what happened, and that she's going to be all right. Come with me into my office," the nurse said, leading Meredith, who turned to her friend.

"Just hang out here for a second, will you, Rachel? I should be right back."

Rachel nodded and came over to the old overstuffed chair where Randy had been sitting.

"Mind if I join you?" she asked the girls.

"It's a free country," said Dee, who wasn't about to give an inch to any friend of Meredith.

"So I gather she's going to be okay," Rachel said. "That's great. Meredith was really worried."

"She *was*?" Andy said, disbelieving.

"Oh yeah," Rachel said. "Meredith is one of the most caring people in the world. But then of course you must already know that."

"Uh, well, she kind of has a way of hiding it around here," Jane said.

"She does give us all little presents almost every day," Maggie said.

"Yes?" Rachel said.

"Yes. Demerit slips and lectures."

Rachel didn't say anything for a minute, then looked at all of them.

"Am I picking up the drift that Meredith is not exactly a big favorite around here?"

"You *could* say that," Dee said.

"Let's put it this way," Andy chimed in. "She makes Hansel and Gretel's witch look like a warm, loving hostess."

Rachel burst out laughing.

"That bad, eh?" She shook her head. "I guess I did see a little of what you're talking about this morning. And I really can't figure out why she'd be so strict with you girls. When she and I were in college together, she was the wildest girl on campus. I heard that for a couple of years after she graduated, they still referred to Social Probation as 'Pembroke Pro.' Dorms couldn't hold her. I remember one night when she tied enough sheets together to climb down from her second story room. Nothing was going to keep her from that Stones concert. So this turnabout just doesn't make any sense. I'd have thought that Meredith would be the most lenient housemother around, that if there were any problem with her in this job, it would be that she was too easy on all of you."

"Hey," Andy said pensively, "maybe that's what *she* figured, too."

"Yeah," Jane said, "maybe — "

But before she could finish her sentence, Meredith and Nurse Zinger were coming out of her office.

"I'll be back at dinnertime when Toby's awake," she was telling the nurse. "There's something I need to talk with her about. Something important."

In the waiting room, the girls exchanged question-mark looks. What did Meredith mean?

CHAPTER SEVENTEEN

Toby woke up completely bewildered. It wasn't morning. She could tell that from the sun setting outside her window. That was another problem. It wasn't her window; this wasn't her room. And on top of it all, what were all these balloons doing here? The room seemed to be filled with them. Red, yellow, blue, green, all tied by strings to a chair at the foot of the bed, fanning up toward the ceiling.

Just then the door to this strange room opened and there were Andy and Jane. Never had there been such a reassuring sight to Toby.

"Is this a dream I'm having and you guys are just characters I'm putting into it?" she asked them.

Andy and Jane both started laughing.

"No, we're real. It's not a dream," Jane told her. "You're in the infirmary. Don't you remember your accident?"

"I got thrown from Maxine and then she ran off," Toby said, mostly to herself, as if she were trying to bring it all back. "Randy came and fetched me. Hey, what's this?" She lifted the blanket off her bandaged leg.

"You sprained your ankle," Andy told her. "The doctor put a cast on it. He says you're not supposed to go to any discos for the next few days. Or do any horseback riding. Or pogo sticking."

Toby nodded, looked at her ankle, and then tried to turn it. "Ouch!"

"Oh yes," Andy added teasingly, "he also said not to do *that*."

Toby stuck out her tongue in response to this, then asked, "Where did all the balloons come from? They're what made me think this might be a dream."

"Neal brought them in from Boston while you were sleeping. We told him how much you love rainbows and so he tried to get them in every color of the rainbow. We added our own little touch of home for you," Jane said, pointing to the ceiling. There between the balloons, taped to the ceiling, was a tea bag.

"Just a loaner until you get back to the dorm," Andy said.

"You guys are the best. And Neal. Neal." Toby punctuated this nonstatement with a sigh.

"He's been downstairs all afternoon," Andy

said. "Seems to be pretty concerned about a particular cowgirl."

Toby went red.

"You must be getting better if you're blushing," Jane teased. "I think it's one of your vital signs, like pulse and breathing."

"So?" Andy asked. "Do you want to see him?"

"How do I look?" Toby asked.

"Like you've been thrown from a horse," Jane said. "A little the worse for wear, but nothing serious."

"I *would* kind of like to see him," Toby admitted shyly.

"No sooner said than done," Jane said, slipping out of the room quietly, then returning noisily with Neal in tow, followed by the shouts of Nurse Zinger from the floor below.

"I'll give him two minutes up there. The last thing a resting girl needs is a guy with that kind of goony romantic look all over his face."

Neal shut the door behind himself and leaned back against it.

"Whew," he sighed. He came over to Toby.

"The balloons are fabulous," she told him. "Some date I am though, eh?"

"Oh, I'm not complaining," he said. "It isn't every day a girl falls head over heels for me."

Toby had to laugh.

"Then you'll give me another chance?" she said.

"Of course," he said. "What about next Saturday? That is, if you're up and around by then."

"Oh, I'll be up," she assured him. "I may not be quite around, though. How would you feel about taking out a girl who's wearing a cast?"

He snapped his fingers in mock disappointment.

"Then we probably won't be able to go free-fall parachuting like I'd planned."

Toby smiled and said, "Would you settle for a lazy night of pizza and a movie?"

"Sold. I'll come by for you at six. Now I'd better get out of here, or that maniac Florence Nightingale is going to yank me out by the ear." He leaned over and kissed Toby softly, then gave a little mock salute of goodbye to Andy and Jane.

"Hmmm," Andy said when he was gone.

"Come on, busybody," Jane said, tugging at her arm. "We've got an important matter to deal with. Any minute now, Zinger is sure to sail in here with a tray of food she's brought straight from the dining hall. Which someone in Toby's weakened condition shouldn't have to face."

"Jane's right," Andy said. "And so we took the liberty of stopping at Wong's and picking up a little Chinese dinner for three." She smiled and shook a huge white paper bag she had set on the floor. "Mongolian beef, anyone? Cashew chicken?" she said, and began opening cartons. Jane set out napkins and soy sauce packets and broke apart everyone's chopsticks. The three roommates feasted through from egg rolls to fortune cookies.

"You pick, Toby," Andy urged, shaking the little waxed paper sack of cookies in front of her roommate. Toby reached in, picked one, cracked it open, and read the fortune. A grin came over her face.

"Come on," Andy urged. "What does it say?"

"You've got to tell us," Jane said. But by now Toby was laughing too hard. It was all she could do to hand the paper slip to them. They each took an end and read it aloud together. WHATEVER THE PLAY, ENJOY BEING IN THE CAST.

This sent them into such gales of laughter that they didn't hear the door to the room open. They were startled when they heard someone clearing her throat in the doorway. It was Meredith.

But a different Meredith from the one they were used to. They could feel the change right away. Part of it was how she looked. For one thing, she wasn't wearing one of her usual severe suits. She just had on old faded jeans and a stretched-out sweat shirt under a paint-splattered down vest. And she wasn't holding her clipboard in front of her, which somehow made her less of a strict authority figure. Like a professor whose lectern has been taken away, she seemed more real and human without her prop.

This new image was not enough to change Toby and Andy and Jane's negative feelings toward Meredith, but it did arouse their curiosity. They let their laughter fall away and sat in silence edged with expectation, watching Meredith.

"Hi," she said to them, in a soft voice they hadn't heard her use before. "I just wanted to check in on Toby. Make sure she's doing all right."

"Probably wants to get her back on her feet so she can stand her up in front of that all-campus board," Jane said under her breath.

"I heard that," Meredith said, then added, "and I probably deserved it. Actually, that's really what I came to talk about. It was this morning, when Randy was bringing you back in, Toby. You were such a mess, and all I could think of was figuring out what rules you were breaking. It was then that I saw how far 'round the bend I'd gone." She took a step into the room. "May I?"

"Oh, sure," Toby said, waving her in. The three roommates waited while Meredith pulled a spare chair over from a corner of the room and sat down nervously on the edge of it. She spoke to Jane and Andy first.

"I heard my friend Rachel let the cat a little ways out of the bag this morning, telling you a bit of my wild and woolly past."

"But we didn't really believe it was true," Andy assured her.

"Oh, but I'm afraid it is. All *too* true. All the way through high school and college, I was the original rebel without a cause. To me, rules were made to be broken, dorms were to sneak out of, teachers and housemothers were to be fooled. I was a rich girl looking for trouble, and I found it. I was in and out of ten schools by the time one of them finally gave me a degree — I think just to get rid of me."

"But what changed you into. . . ." Toby paused, trying to think of some tactful way to phrase it. ". . . into the way you are now?"

"My father died and my mother got sick and the money ran out. Suddenly I had to find a job, and keep it. My mother's family is friendly with Ms. Allardyce's, and so she gave me a chance. But I knew she knew about my history, and so I thought I'd better prove that I was not only not a troublemaker myself, but wouldn't allow trouble in my dorm. I memorized the Canby Hall rule book and was determined to show I'd crack down on every possible infraction."

"Oh, I think you succeeded at that," Andy said.

"Yeah," Meredith said ruefully, "but to

what point? Every girl in Baker hates me, and I don't think Ms. Allardyce was any too happy when I brought in my list of girls with enough demerits to go before the all-campus board."

"How many were on the list?" Jane asked.

"Seventy-two," Meredith admitted sheepishly, and held up a hand. "I know, I know, it's ghastly. I could tell when all the color drained out of Ms. Allardyce's face and she said that the board was used to handling one or two cases a term, and that at this rate some of the girls wouldn't come up before the board until they were in their forties."

The roommates smiled at the thought of this.

"Can you just see Andy?" Jane said. "She'll be sitting with her husband and two kids at breakfast one morning, just about to run off to rehearsals for the ballet she'll be starring in, and all of a sudden she'll slap her forehead and say, 'Oh my! It's my day to go back to Canby Hall and stand before the all-campus board!' "

Everyone laughed at this, including Meredith.

"I know it's ridiculous. I went way too far. I can see that now. But how can I go back? With all the girls hating me like they do. . . ."

"I'm not sure they hate you so much as they're afraid of you," Toby said. Which prompted Andy to offer her own analysis.

"Plus they think that if you're so strict with

us, you must be kind of a goody-goody your-self. I think if they knew you really aren't like that, it would be a start."

"But while everyone's sitting under such an avalanche of demerits, I don't really think they can possibly work up much in the way of good feelings toward you," Jane countered.

Meredith nodded.

"Jane's right. I've got to wipe the slate clean and start over. But how? I can't take back each and every demerit I gave out."

"Why not?" Andy said. "Why not have an Amnesty Day, like the library does when they want to get back all those books people have been holding on to for years because they're afraid if they bring them in, they'll get a jillion-dollar fine?"

"Amnesty Day? Hmmm," Meredith mused. "You know, it just might work."

"Meredith?" Toby said shyly, then paused to ask, "Is it all right if I call you that?"

"Call me Merry."

"Well, I just want to say that you think this is going to be so hard, starting over with the girls of Baker House, but look how easy it was with us. We just need to know that you're not against us. The other girls will feel the same way. What you've got going for you is that they *want* to like you. We're all used to hav-ing a housemother we really love. It's one of the best things about Baker."

"Yes," Meredith said with defeat in her

voice, "but I'll never have Alison's place in your hearts."

"That's true," Jane admitted. "But you can make a new place for yourself. A Meredith place."

"And another great thing about being a little more relaxed around here is that the girls in Baker are basically a pretty good bunch," Andy said. "You really don't have to give us demerits to keep us in line. Your new life here is going to be so much easier without all those pink slips. Just think of the time you'll save in paperwork alone. We'll have to install a hammock up in The Penthouse so you'll have someplace to spend all your new hours of leisure."

Meredith smiled and stood up.

"You three are great. Of course, Alison told me as much before she left. She said if I ever needed special friends in Baker, to look in 407."

"She said that?" Toby asked. "Really?"

"Aw shucks," Andy said mockingly, but it was clear she was pleased.

"Well, if you really mean what you've been telling us," Jane said, "you can count on at least the three of us being behind the new, improved Meredith Pembroke!"

By Monday, the rumor mill had spread Meredith's true story through every room of Baker House. The place was buzzing with curiosity about the housemother and the supposed Amnesty Day.

After breakfast, Andy and Jane were walking at a snail's pace up the front steps of the dorm, keeping pace with Toby, who was slowed down considerably by her crutches. When they got into the front lobby, they could see a crowd at the door of the mailroom. They found their way inside and got to the bulletin board, which was the focus of everyone's attention. There were two freshly typed notices tacked up on it. The first read:

FROM: Meredith Pembroke
TO: All Residents of Baker House
Tuesday will be Amnesty Day. All demerits turned in to the housemother before midnight will be destroyed and forever forgotten.

The second notice said:

FROM: Merry
TO: Her Girls
Some of you may have heard a rumor that when I was in college, I slid down two stories on tied-together sheets to sneak out to a Rolling Stones concert. The story is false. It was a Led Zeppelin concert.

Well," said Andy as she and Jane ran interference for Toby on their way out of the

crowded mailroom, "looks like we've got ourselves a *new* new housemother!"

*Someone is making trouble for the girls of
407. Can anyone be trusted? Read The Girls
of Canby Hall #22,* TROUBLEMAKER.